BLUEBONNET at the Alamo

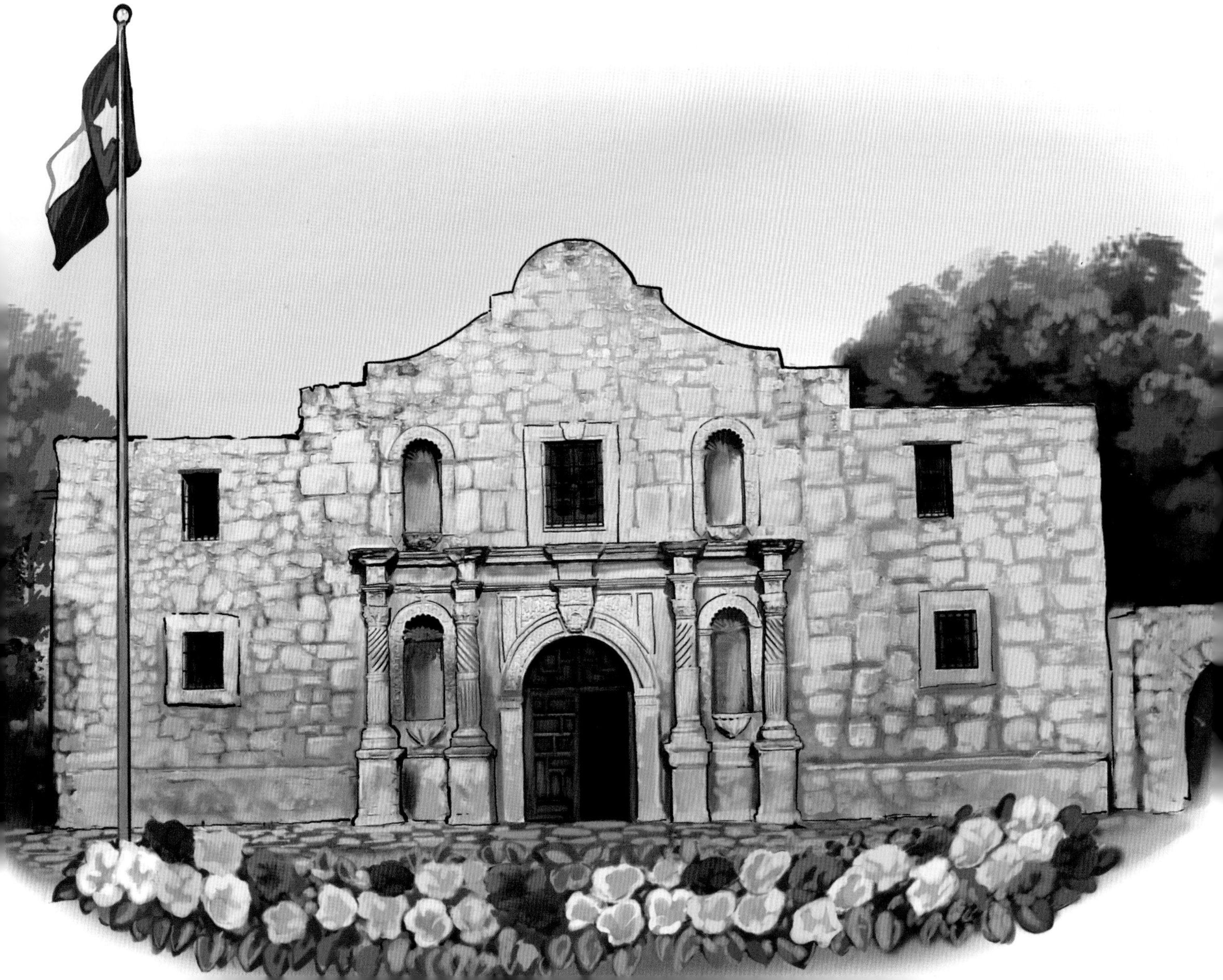

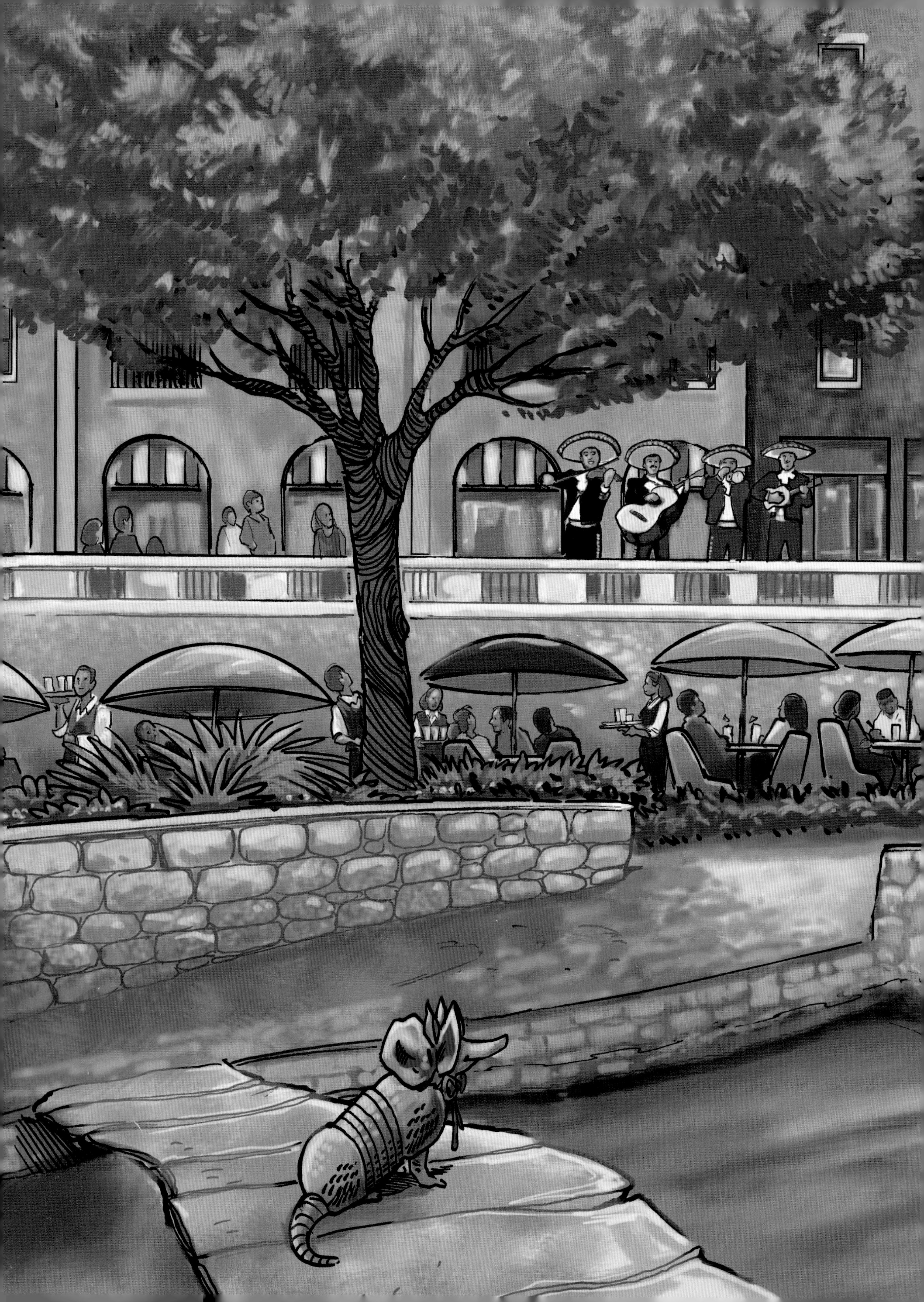

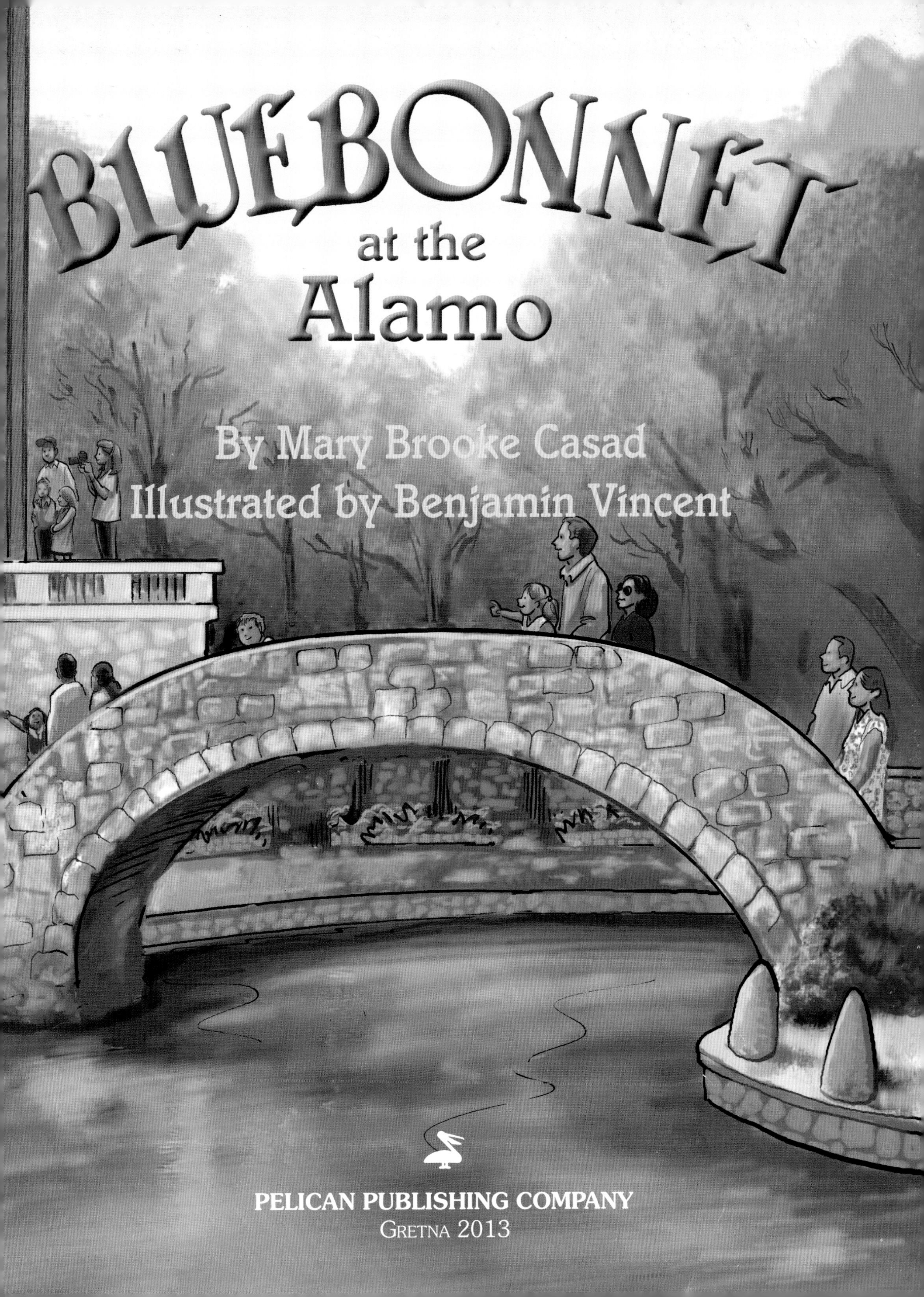

BLUEBONNET at the Alamo

By Mary Brooke Casad

Illustrated by Benjamin Vincent

PELICAN PUBLISHING COMPANY
GRETNA 2013

For "Mimi," my grandmother Mary G. Kelley,
who taught me to always "Remember the Alamo!"

The word "Pelican" and the depiction of a pelican are trademarks of Pelican Publishing Company, Inc., and are registered in the U.S. Patent and Trademark Office.

Library of Congress Cataloging-in-Publication Data

Casad, Mary Brooke.
  Bluebonnet at the Alamo / by Mary Brooke Casad ; illustrated by Benjamin Vincent.
       pages cm
  Summary: "While visiting the Alamo in San Antonio, Bluebonnet the armadillo meets another armadillo, whose family has lived there since the days of the famous battle. In fact, this armadillo has Jim Bowie's knife. Can Bluebonnet convince him to leave it to the Alamo Museum so that the public can view it?"— Provided by publisher.
  ISBN 978-1-4556-1806-4 (hardcover : alk. paper) — ISBN 978-1-4556-1807-1 (e-book) 1. Alamo (San Antonio, Tex.)—Juvenile fiction. [1. Alamo (San Antonio, Tex.)—Fiction. 2. Texas—Fiction. 3. Armadillos—Fiction.] I. Vincent, Benjamin, illustrator. II. Title.
  PZ7.C265Bmh 2013
  [E]—dc23
                                    2013012630

Printed in Malaysia
Published by Pelican Publishing Company, Inc.
1000 Burmaster Street, Gretna, Louisiana 70053

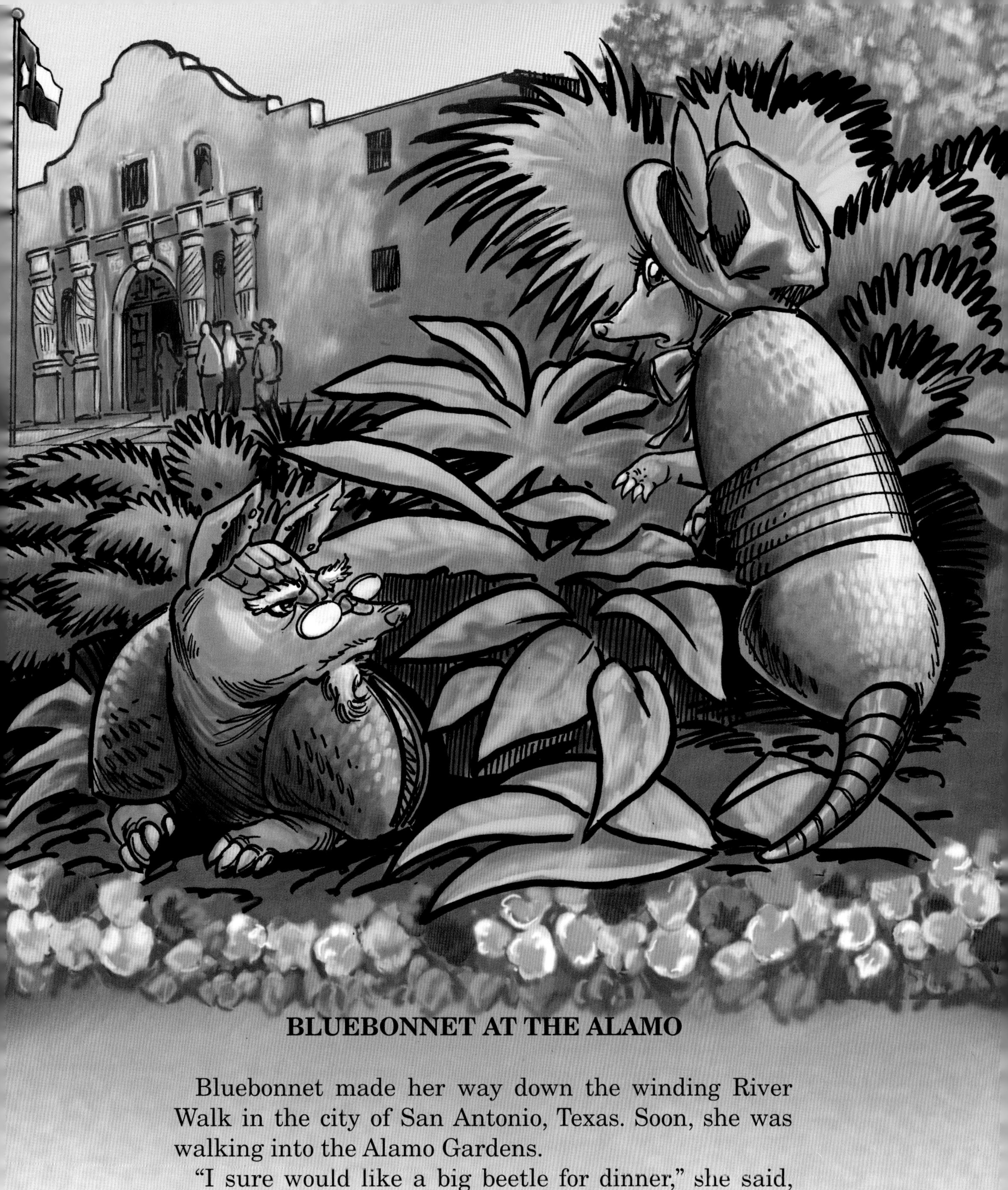

BLUEBONNET AT THE ALAMO

Bluebonnet made her way down the winding River Walk in the city of San Antonio, Texas. Soon, she was walking into the Alamo Gardens.

"I sure would like a big beetle for dinner," she said, digging into the earth with her claws. Suddenly, Bluebonnet heard a rustling in the bushes. Peering out from beneath her sunbonnet, she saw another armadillo.

"Well, young lady, just what do you think you're doing?" he asked gruffly.

"I'm searching for my supper, sir," said Bluebonnet shyly.

"Humph!" he snorted. "Well, you won't find any there, although I know of a place where you will find some. Just what did you say your name was?"

"I'm Bluebonnet," she replied. "I've come to see the Alamo."

"First time here, eh?" he asked. "Well, I can tell you all about it. Permit me to introduce myself. I'm Digger Diller."

"Have you lived here long?" she asked.

"Long? Why, I've lived here all my life," Digger Diller said proudly. "My family has been here for generations. In fact, my great-great-grand-diller was here during the Battle of the Alamo, when Texas was fighting for her independence from Mexico."

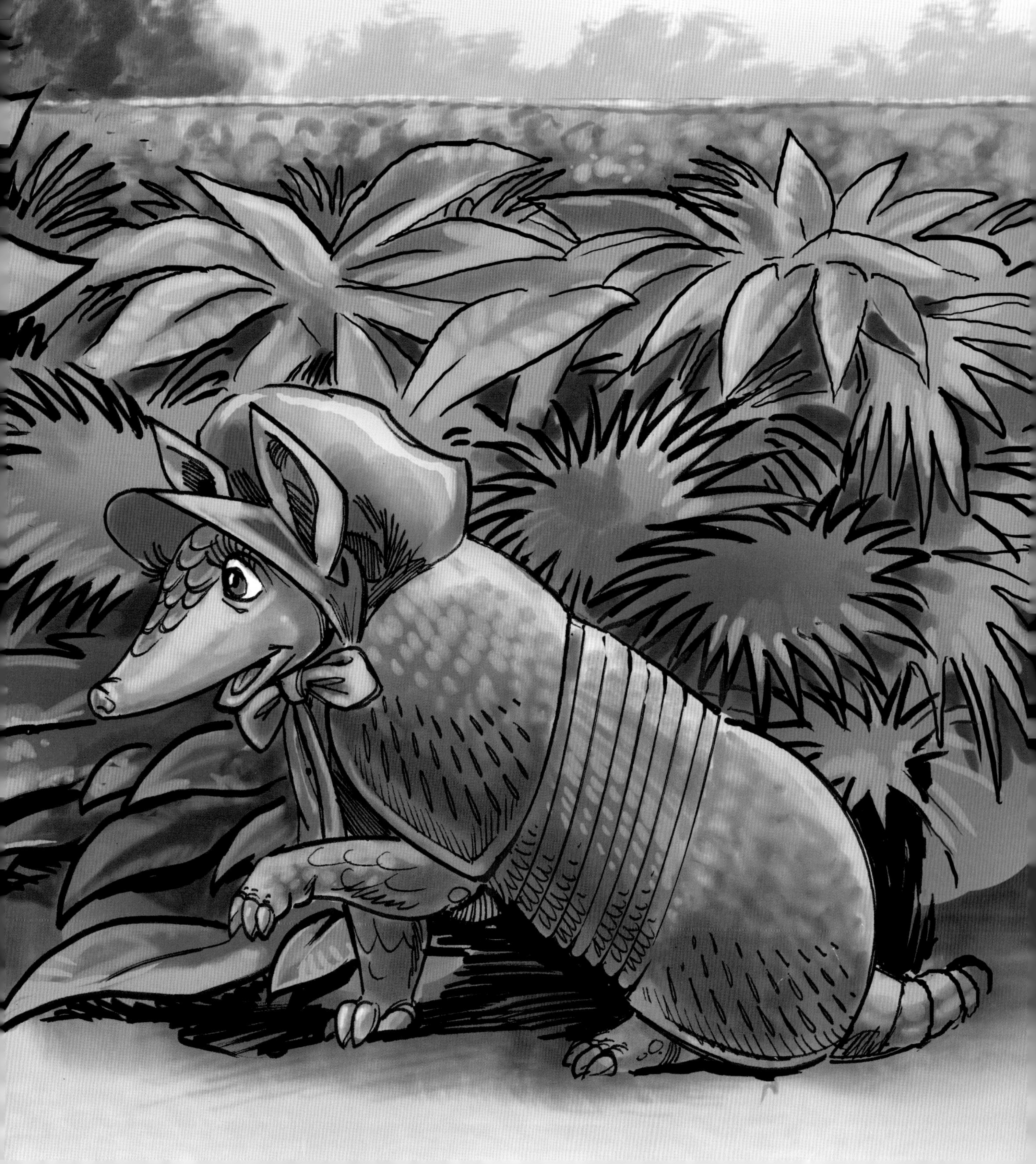

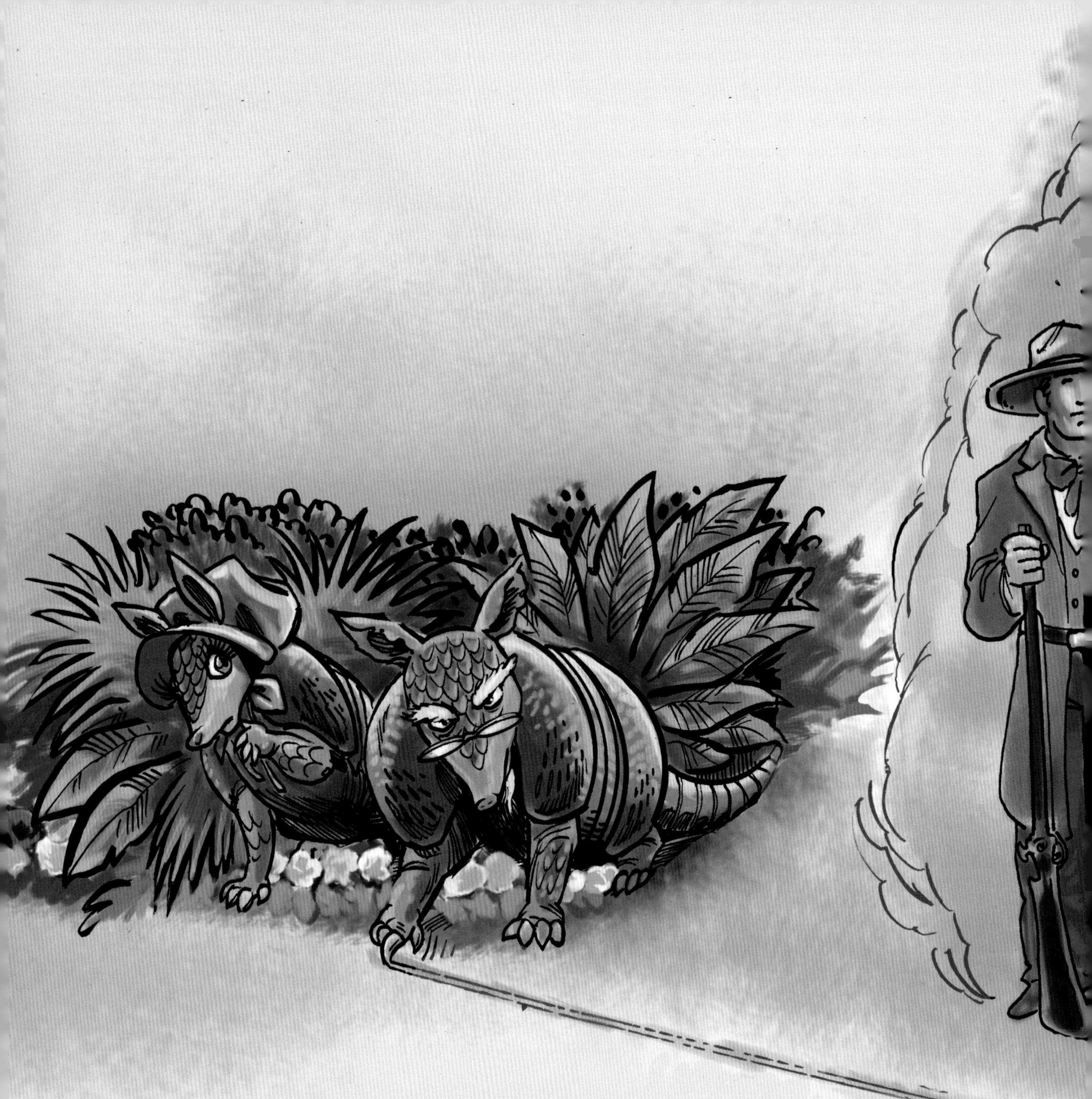

"What did Great-Great-Grand-Diller see?" Bluebonnet asked eagerly.

"The army of Mexican general Antonio López de Santa Anna arrived in San Antonio on February 23, 1836," said Digger Diller. "The Alamo would be under siege for thirteen days. 'Alamo' is the Spanish word for 'cottonwood.' It was once a Spanish mission but became a fortress the Texans defended with their lives."

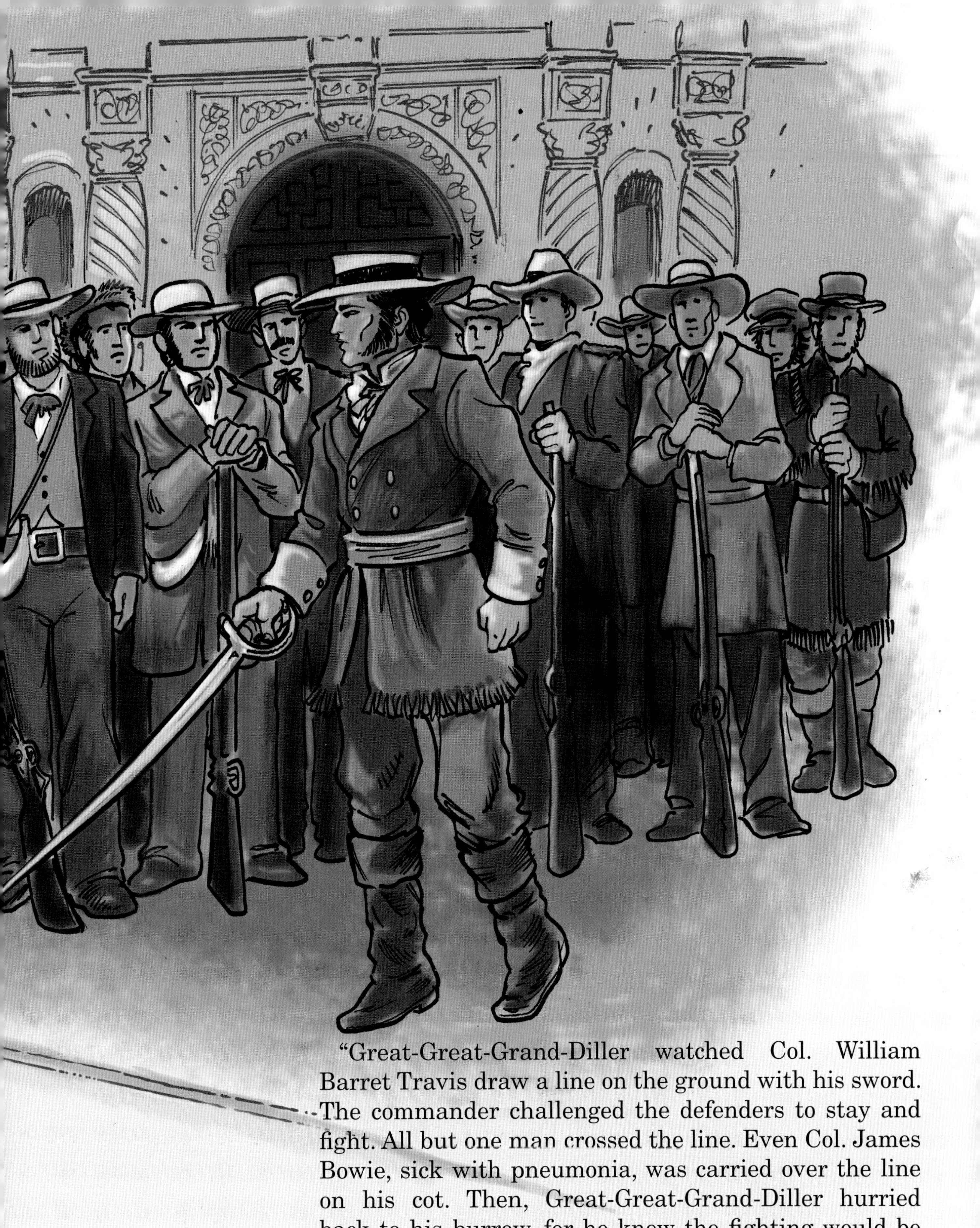

"Great-Great-Grand-Diller watched Col. William Barret Travis draw a line on the ground with his sword. The commander challenged the defenders to stay and fight. All but one man crossed the line. Even Col. James Bowie, sick with pneumonia, was carried over the line on his cot. Then, Great-Great-Grand-Diller hurried back to his burrow, for he knew the fighting would be fierce. Beneath the ground in his diller den, he could hear the bugles sound. The burrow shook every time the cannonballs hit the fortress walls."

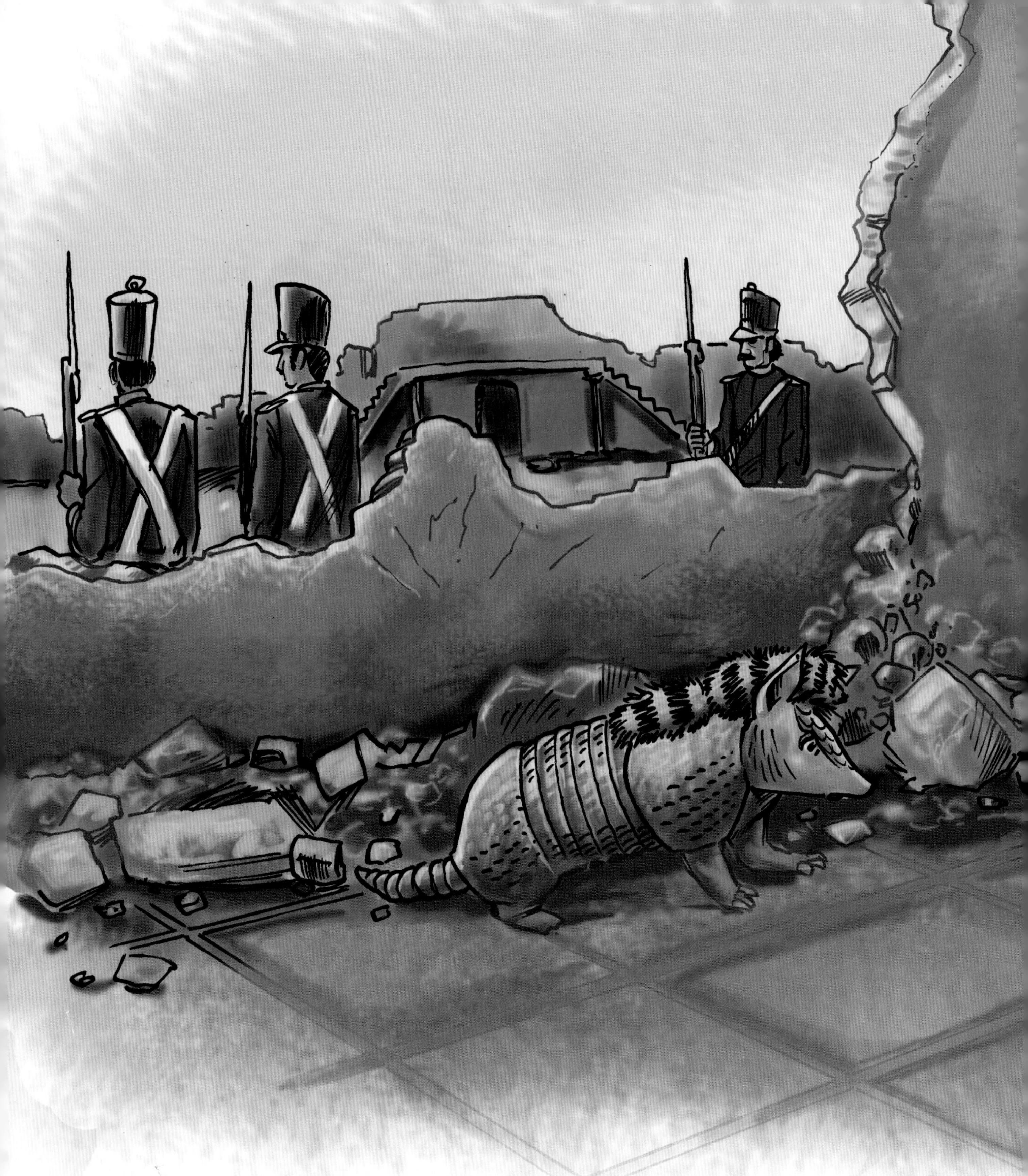

"When did he come out of his burrow?" asked Bluebonnet.

"March 6, 1836," said Digger Diller. "The final battle took place at daybreak. When all was quiet, Great-Great-Grand Diller crept out. Mexican soldiers now stood guard over the Alamo."

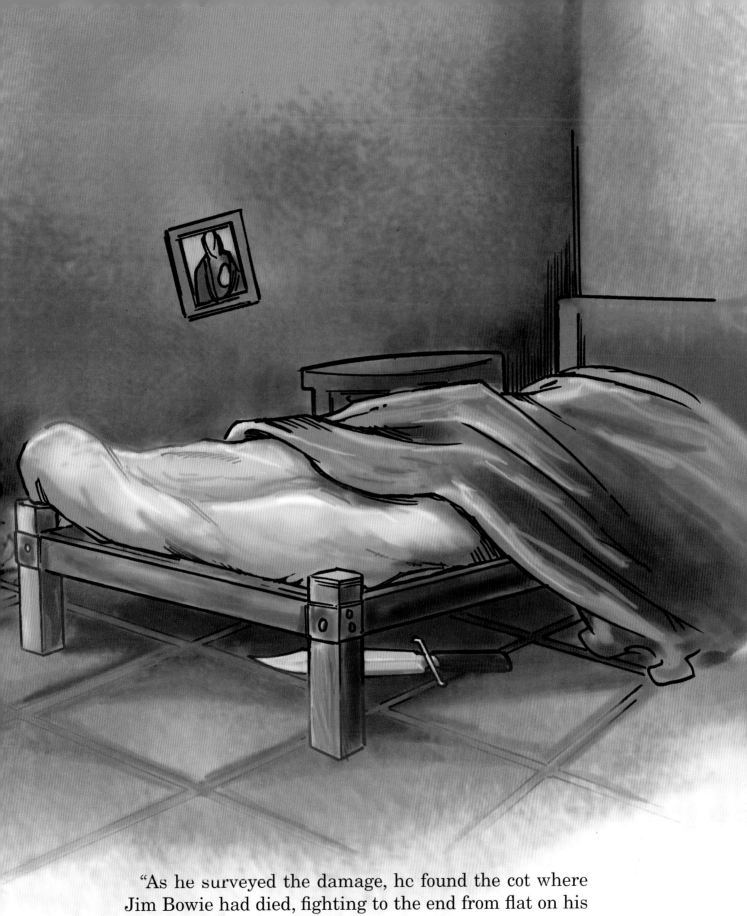

"As he surveyed the damage, hc found the cot where Jim Bowie had died, fighting to the end from flat on his back. Beneath the cot lay Jim Bowie's knife, a knife made for him and named for him."

He looked around, making sure they were alone, then whispered in her ear, "Would you like to see it?"

"You mean you have Jim Bowie's knife?" Bluebonnet asked excitedly.

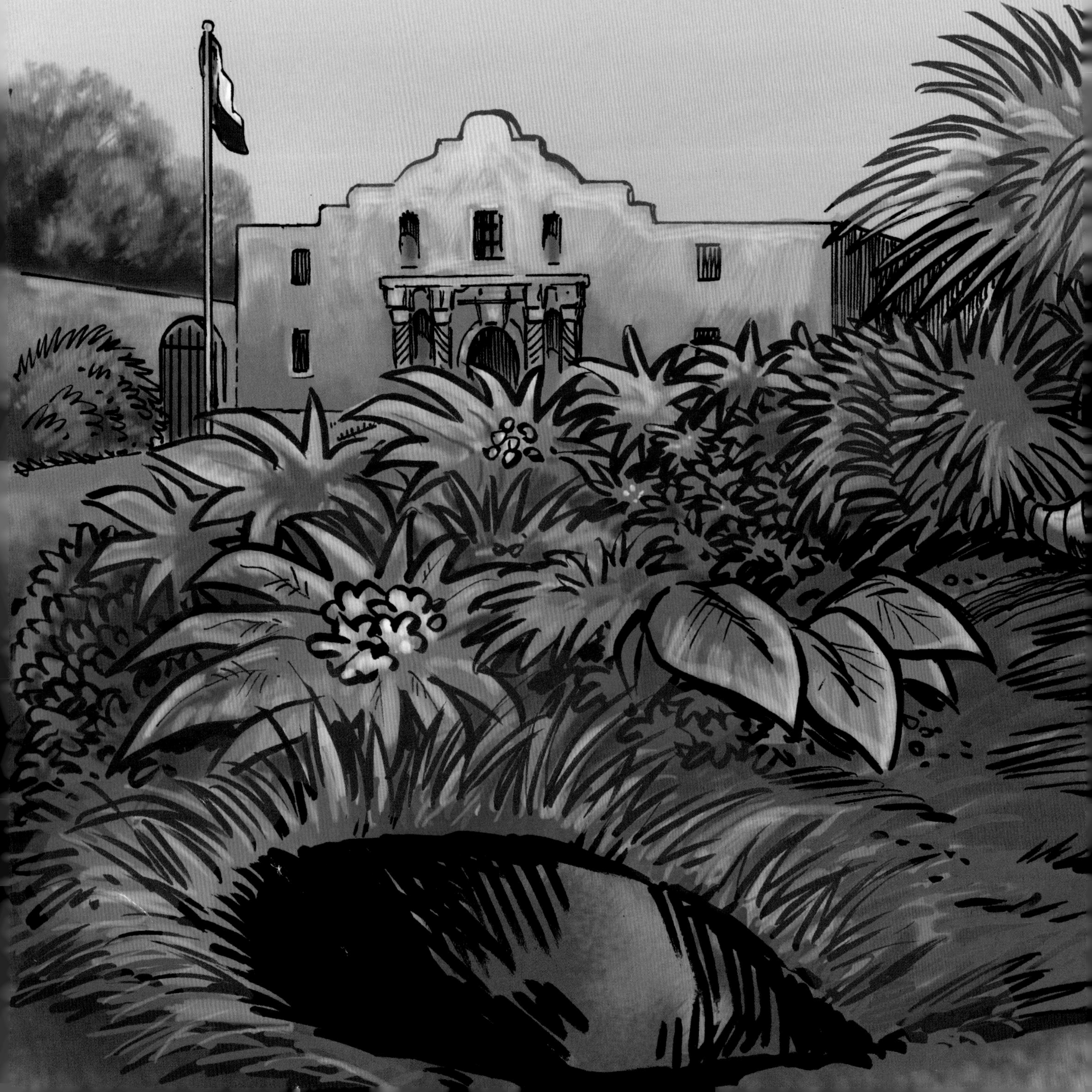

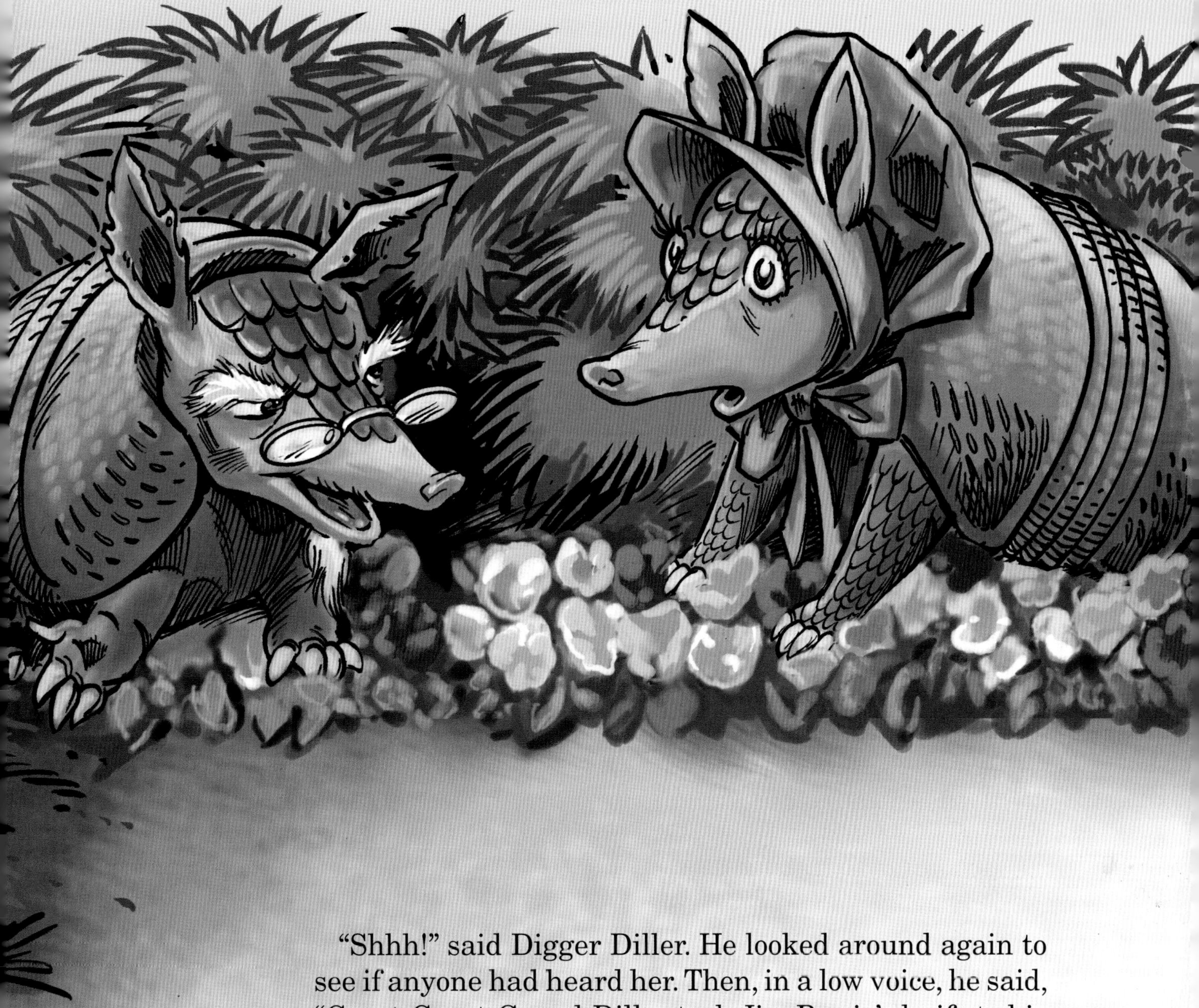

"Shhh!" said Digger Diller. He looked around again to see if anyone had heard her. Then, in a low voice, he said, "Great-Great-Grand-Diller took Jim Bowie's knife to his burrow. It's our family secret, but I'll show it to you if you like."

Digger Diller turned and rambled off, and Bluebonnet quickly followed. Inside his burrow, he showed Bluebonnet the old knife that had been hidden for more than one hundred years.

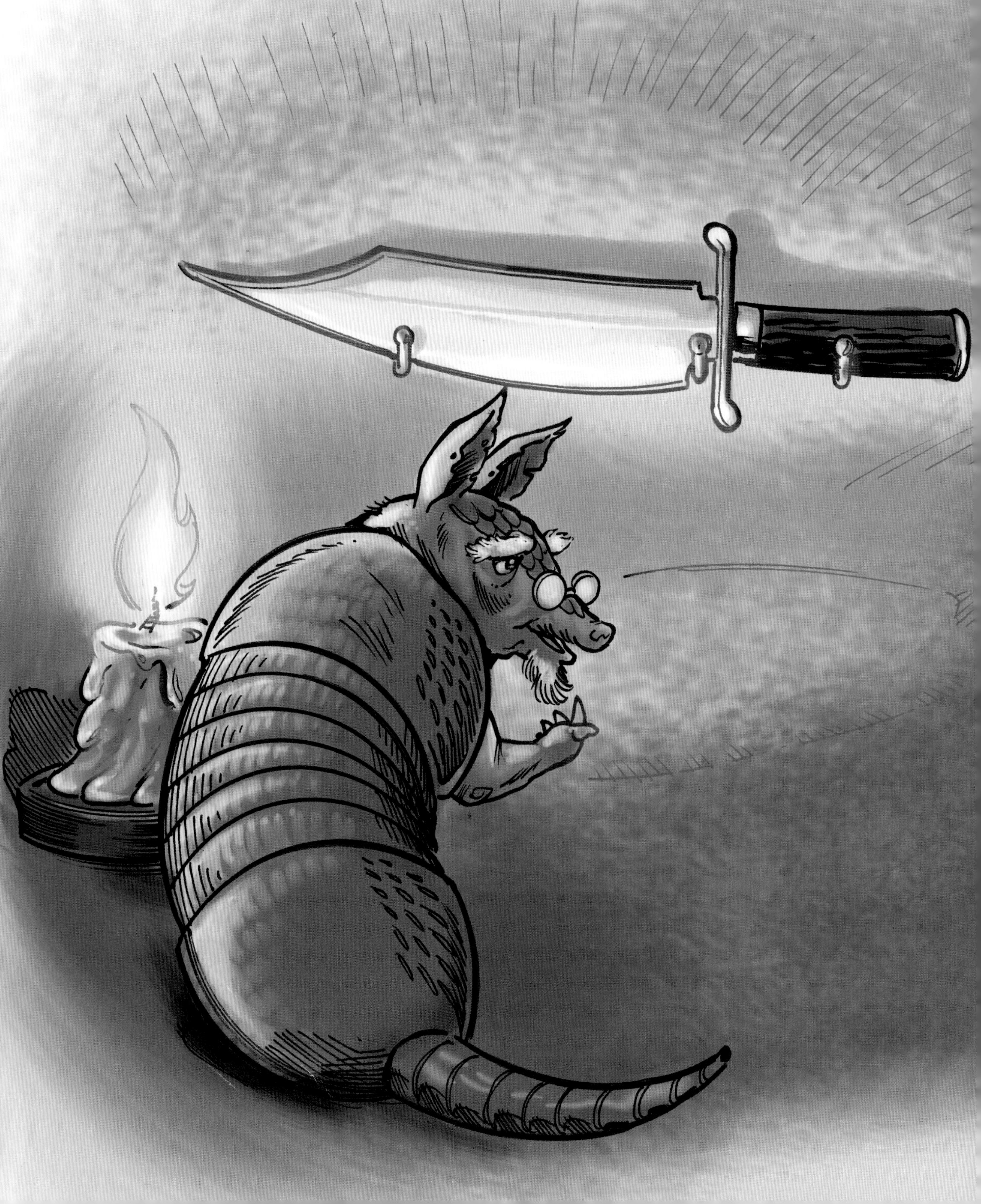

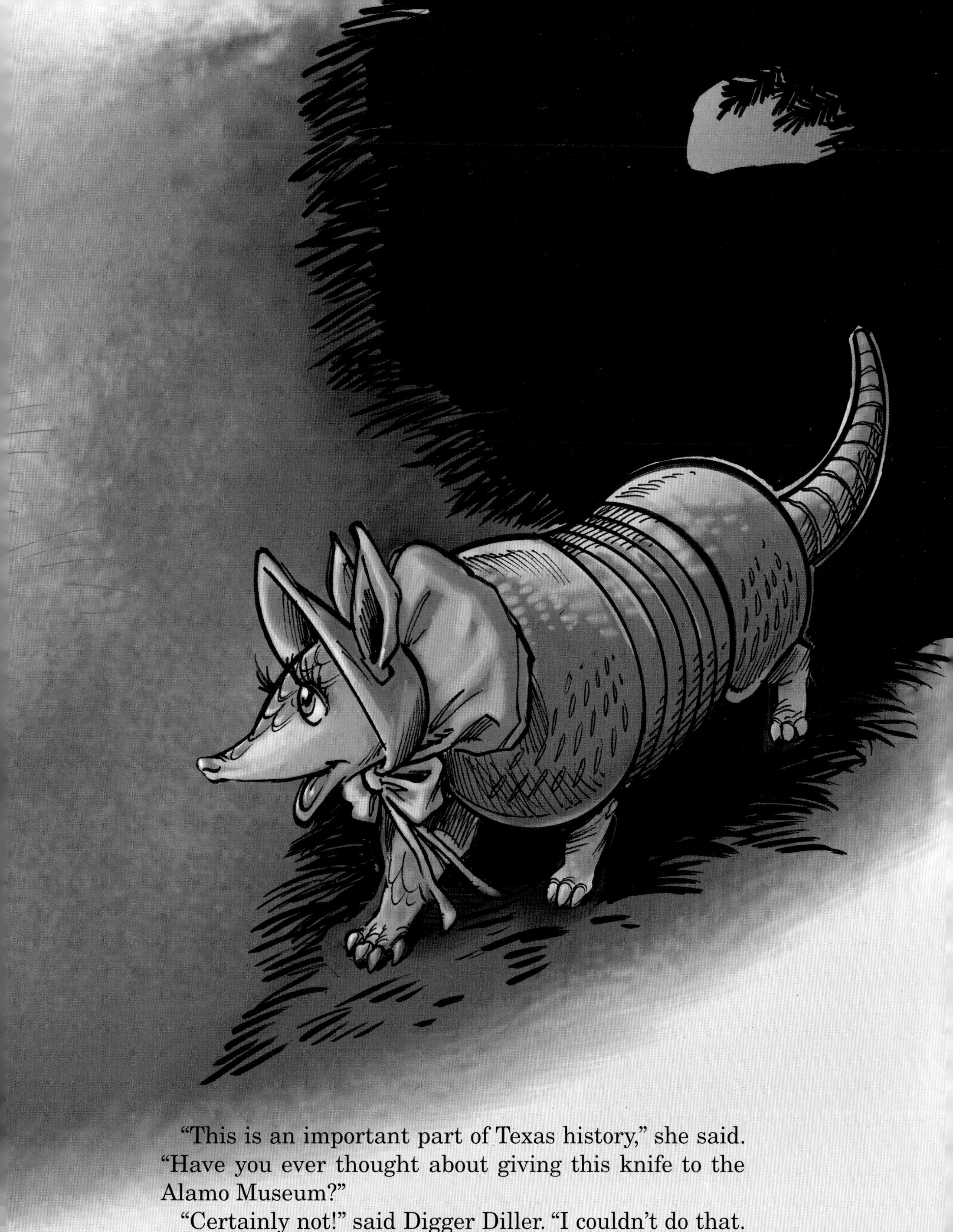

"This is an important part of Texas history," she said. "Have you ever thought about giving this knife to the Alamo Museum?"

"Certainly not!" said Digger Diller. "I couldn't do that. Why, this knife is a family heirloom."

"Yes," said Bluebonnet, "but it's also a treasure belonging to all Texans. Just think what it would mean to the visitors who come to learn about Alamo history. You could make it possible for them to see Jim Bowie's knife."

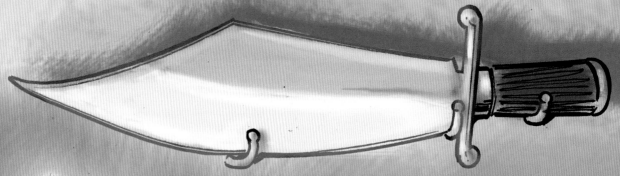

Digger Diller scratched his head. "Hmmmm," he said. "Well, now, I never thought about that before. How could I give them the knife?"

"We could leave the knife in front of the museum door," said Bluebonnet. "We can watch to make sure the museum keeper finds it."

"I guess that would work. I just don't know what Great-Great-Grand-Diller would say about this," he added, shaking his head.

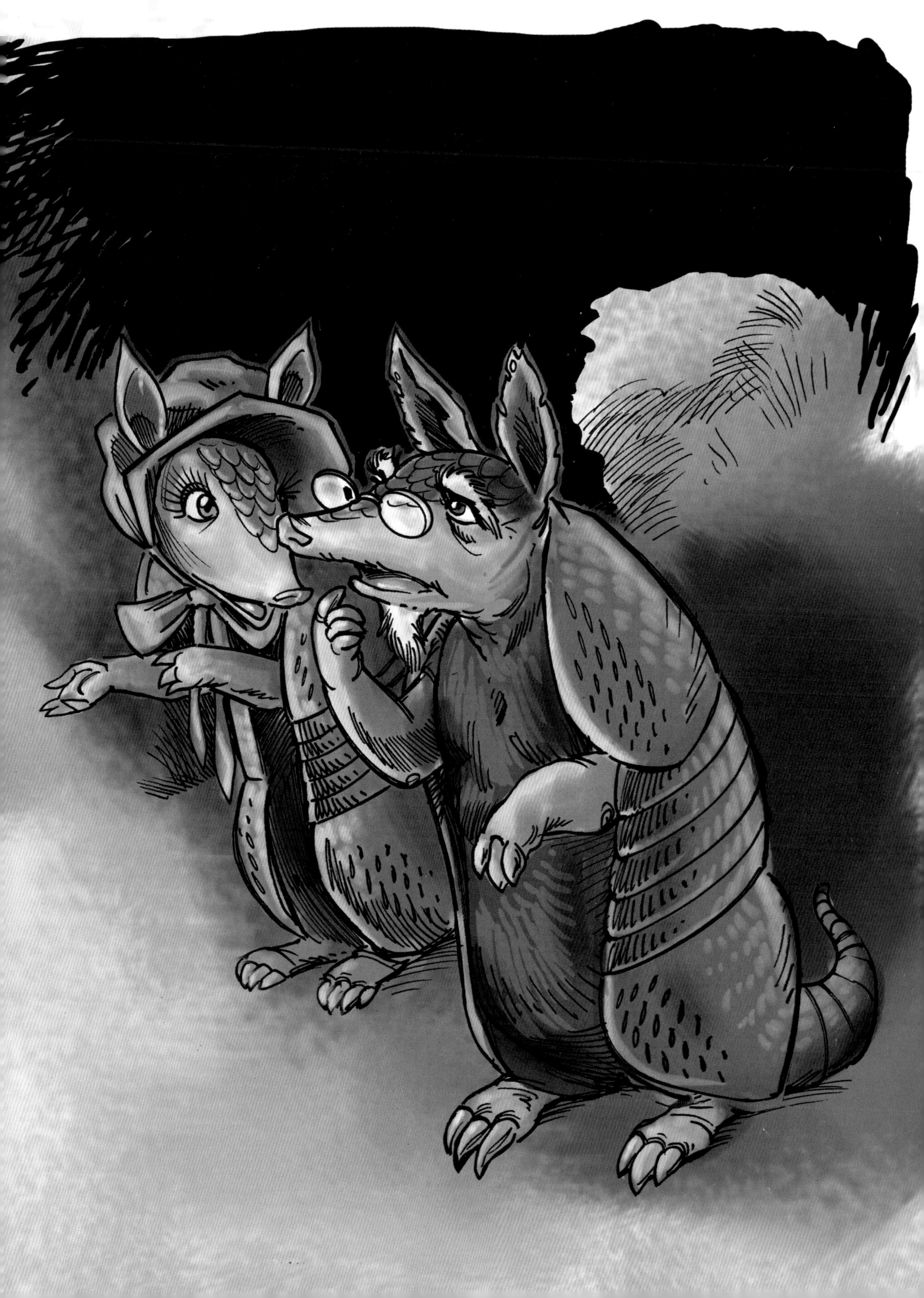

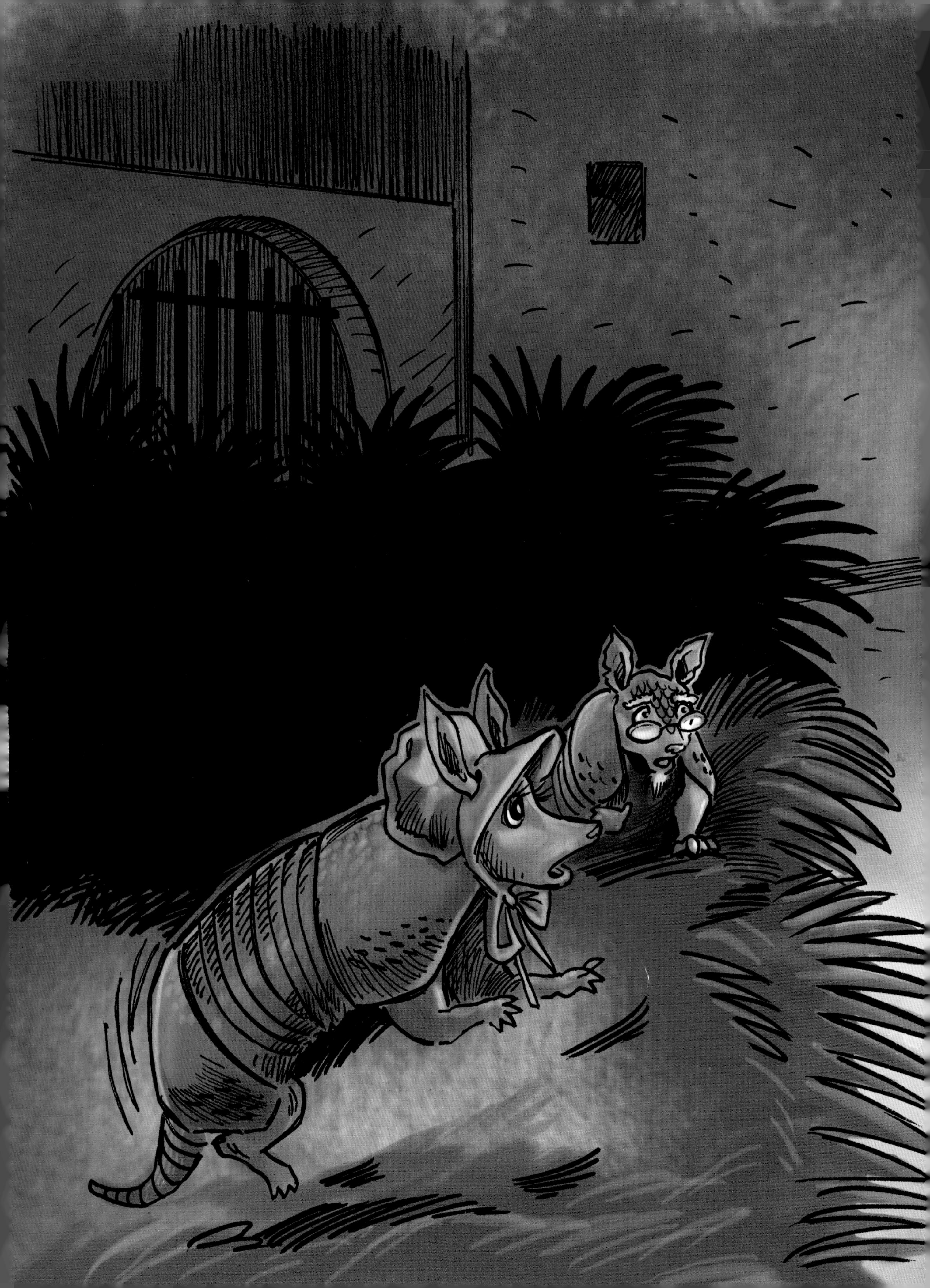

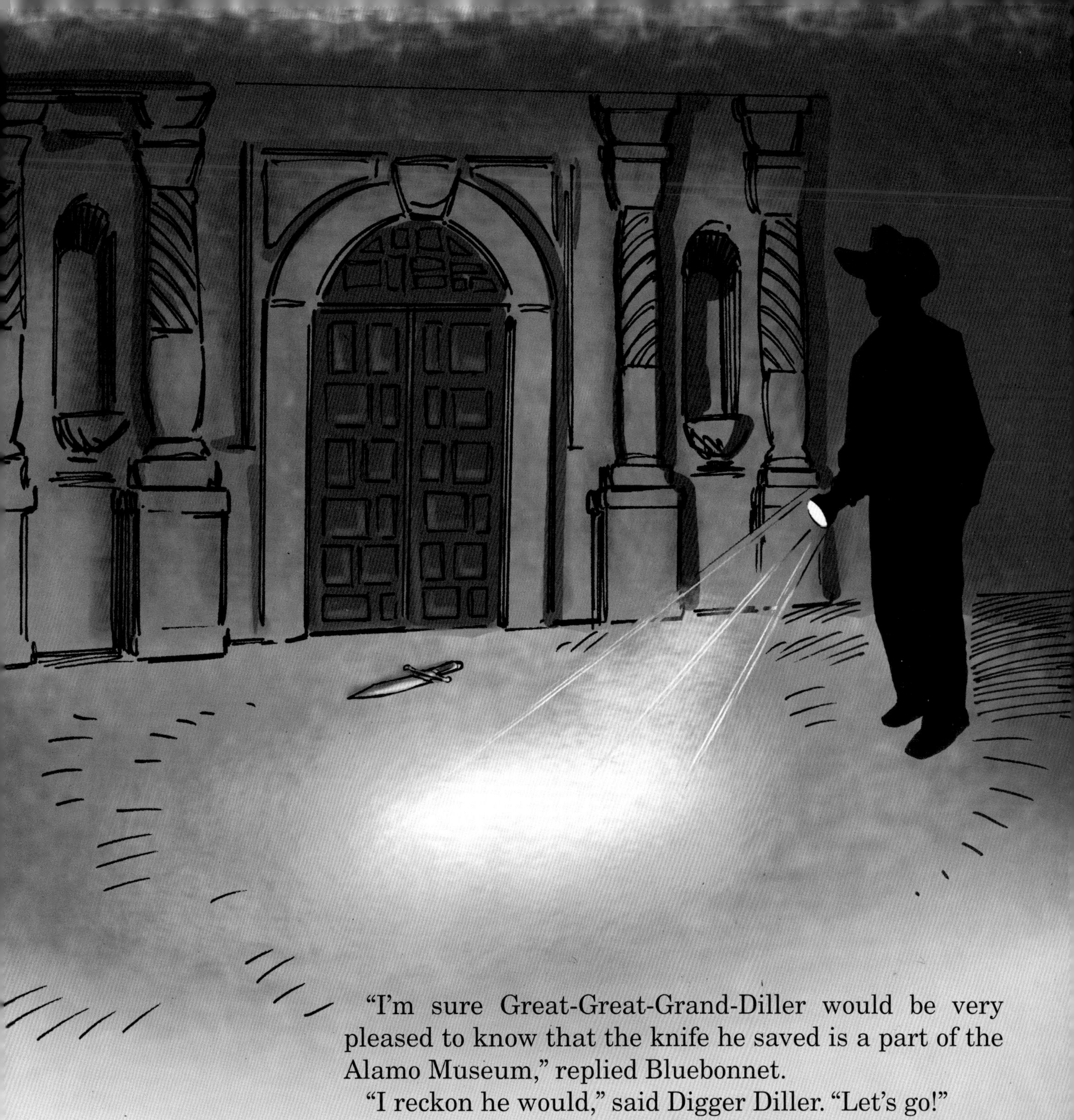

"I'm sure Great-Great-Grand-Diller would be very pleased to know that the knife he saved is a part of the Alamo Museum," replied Bluebonnet.

"I reckon he would," said Digger Diller. "Let's go!"

Bluebonnet followed him out of the burrow. Digger Diller left the knife by the front door of the museum. Then, the two armadillos hid nearby.

They waited and waited. Bluebonnet grew sleepy. Digger Diller yawned.

Suddenly, they saw a movement in the shadows. Bluebonnet was so startled she jumped straight up into the air!

A security guard walked up to the door and checked the lock. As he turned away, he noticed the knife.

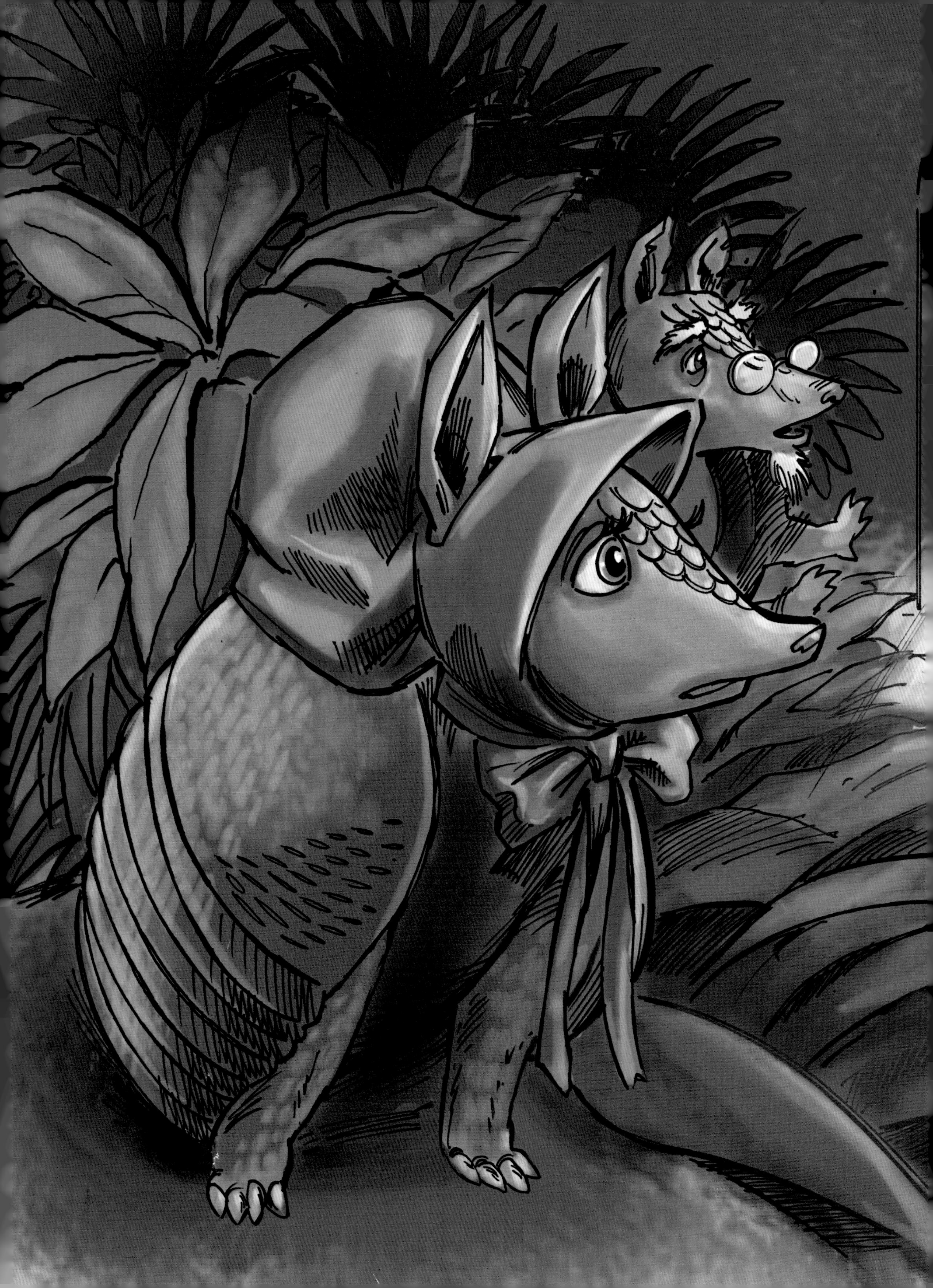

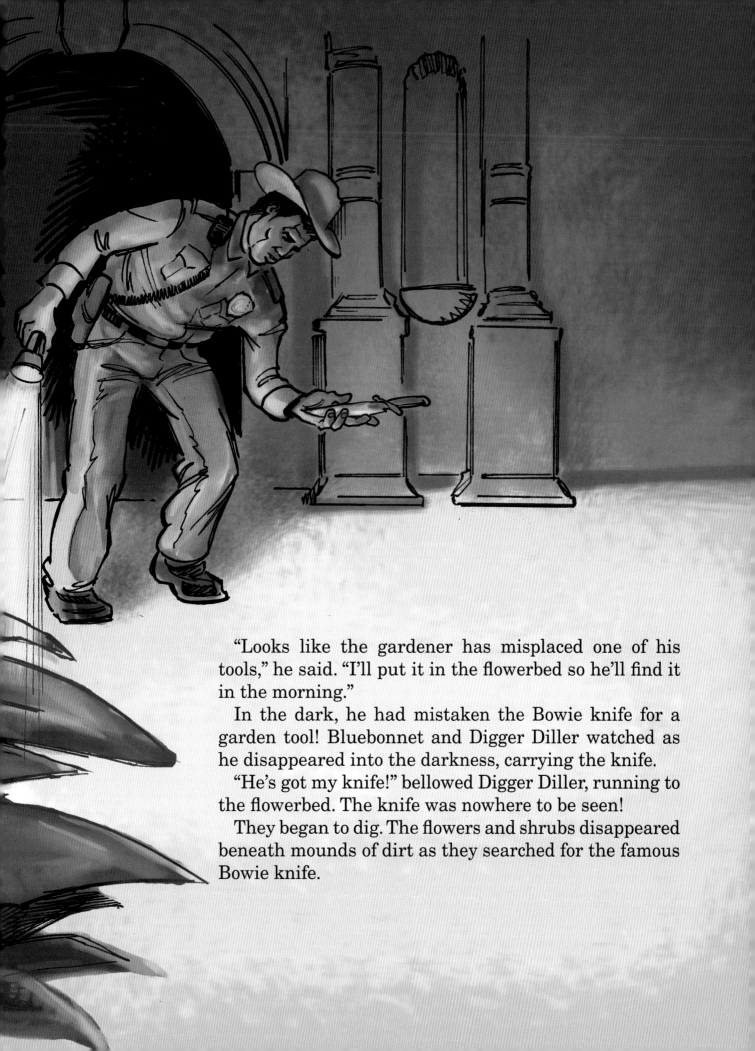

"Looks like the gardener has misplaced one of his tools," he said. "I'll put it in the flowerbed so he'll find it in the morning."

In the dark, he had mistaken the Bowie knife for a garden tool! Bluebonnet and Digger Diller watched as he disappeared into the darkness, carrying the knife.

"He's got my knife!" bellowed Digger Diller, running to the flowerbed. The knife was nowhere to be seen!

They began to dig. The flowers and shrubs disappeared beneath mounds of dirt as they searched for the famous Bowie knife.

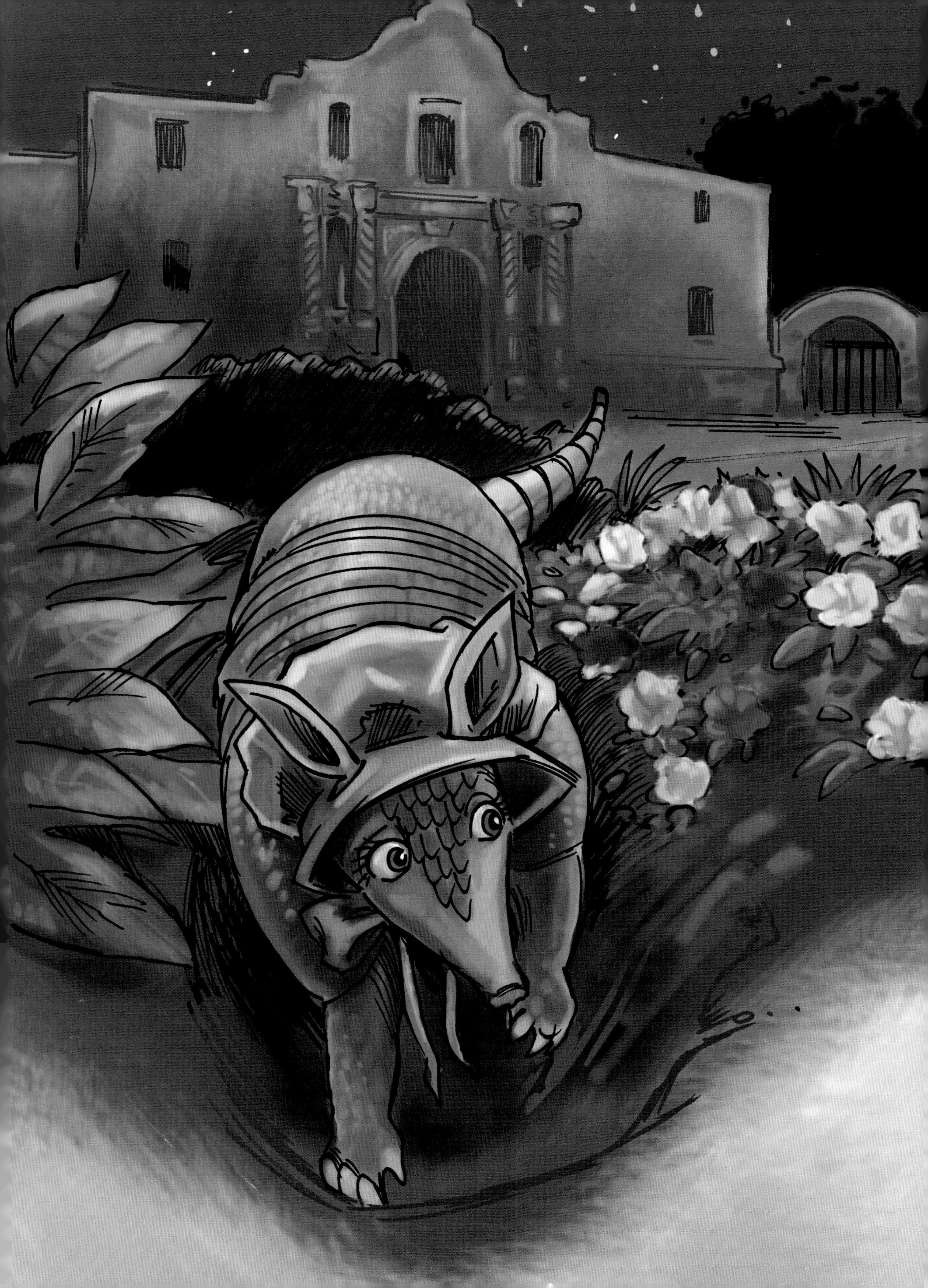

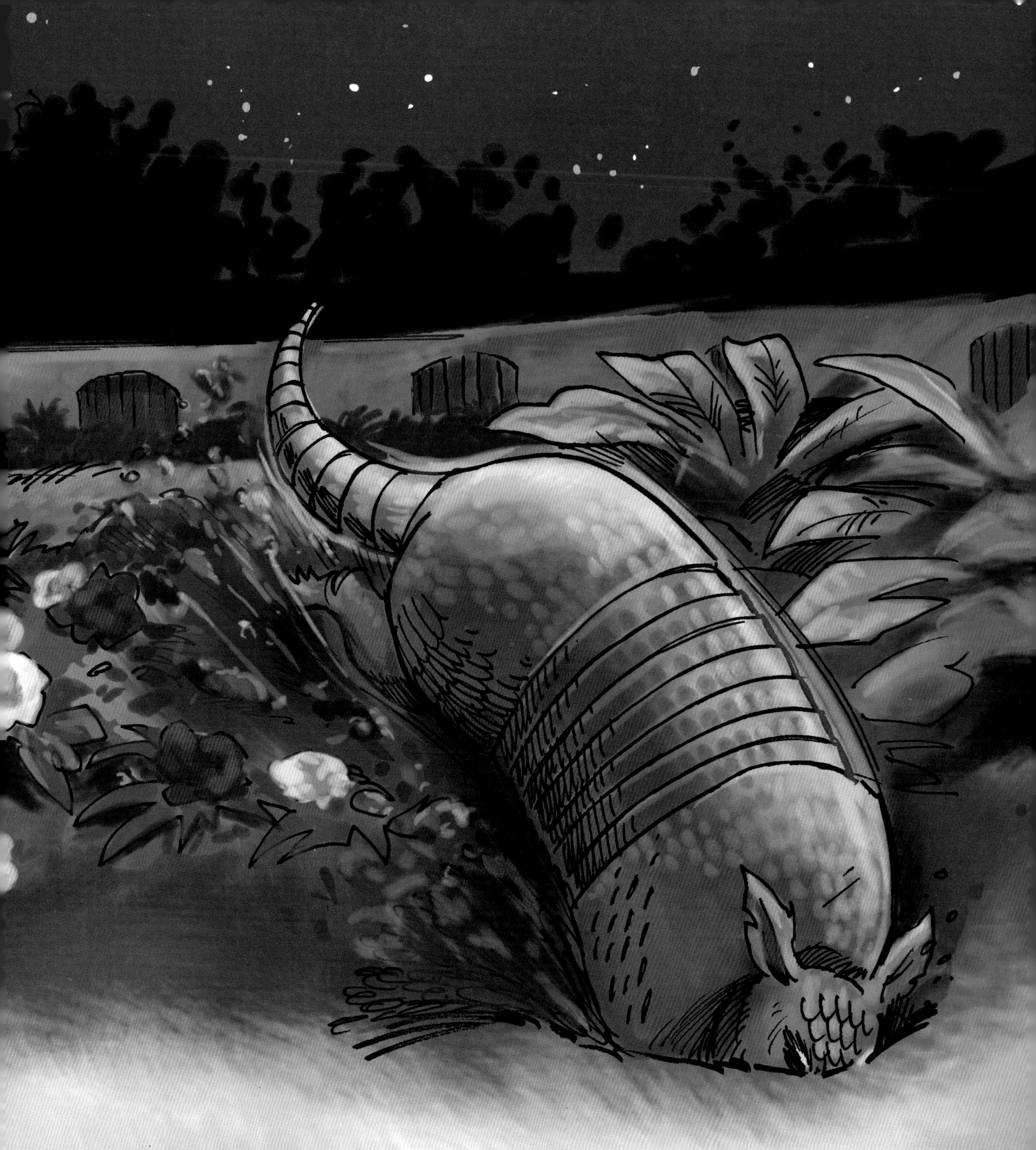

"See what a mess you've gotten me into," said Digger Diller, who was digging so fast that Bluebonnet knew why he was called Digger. "I've lost the Bowie knife that's been in our family for generations. It was our great pride, our special secret. Now it's gone. And it's all your fault."

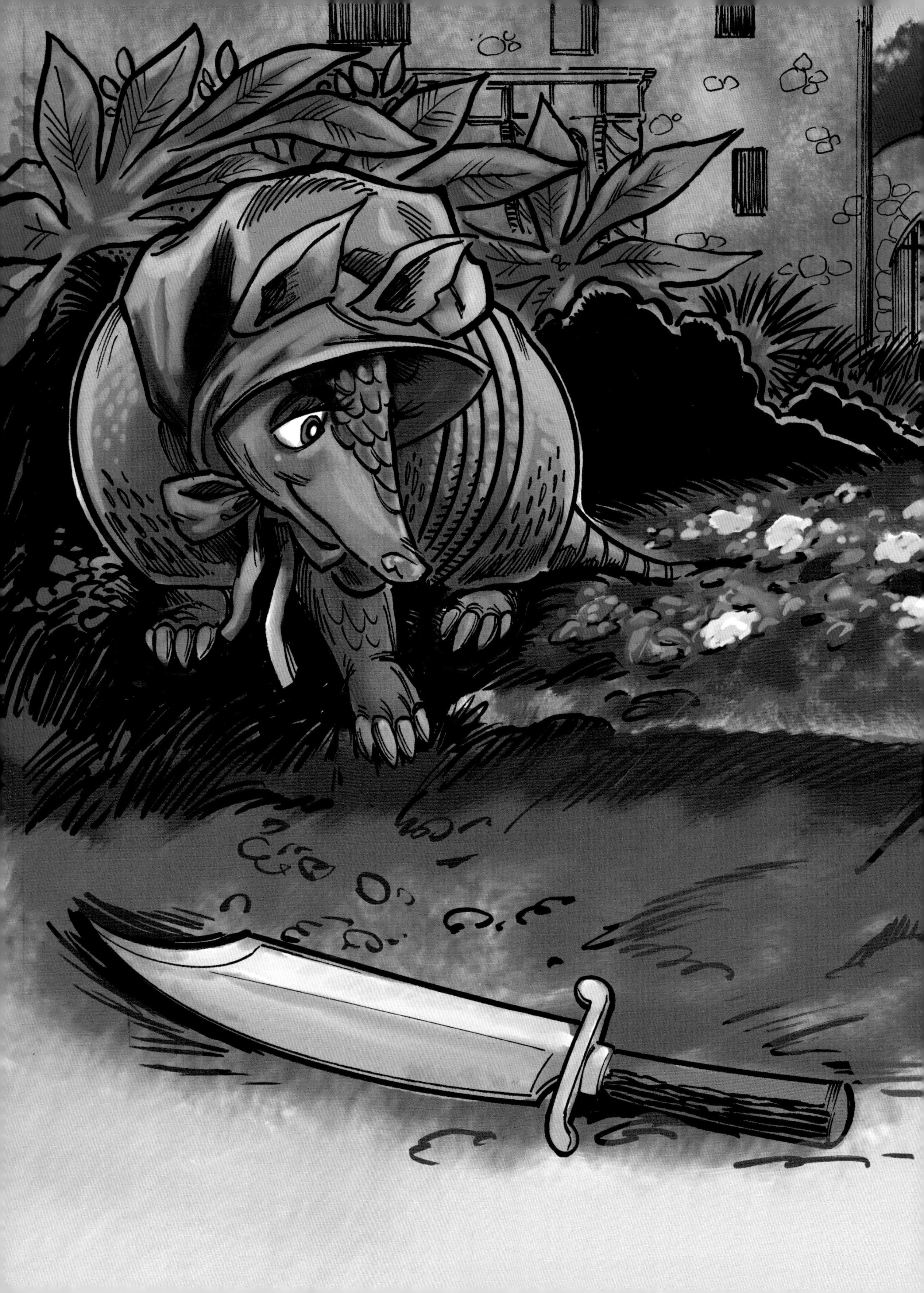

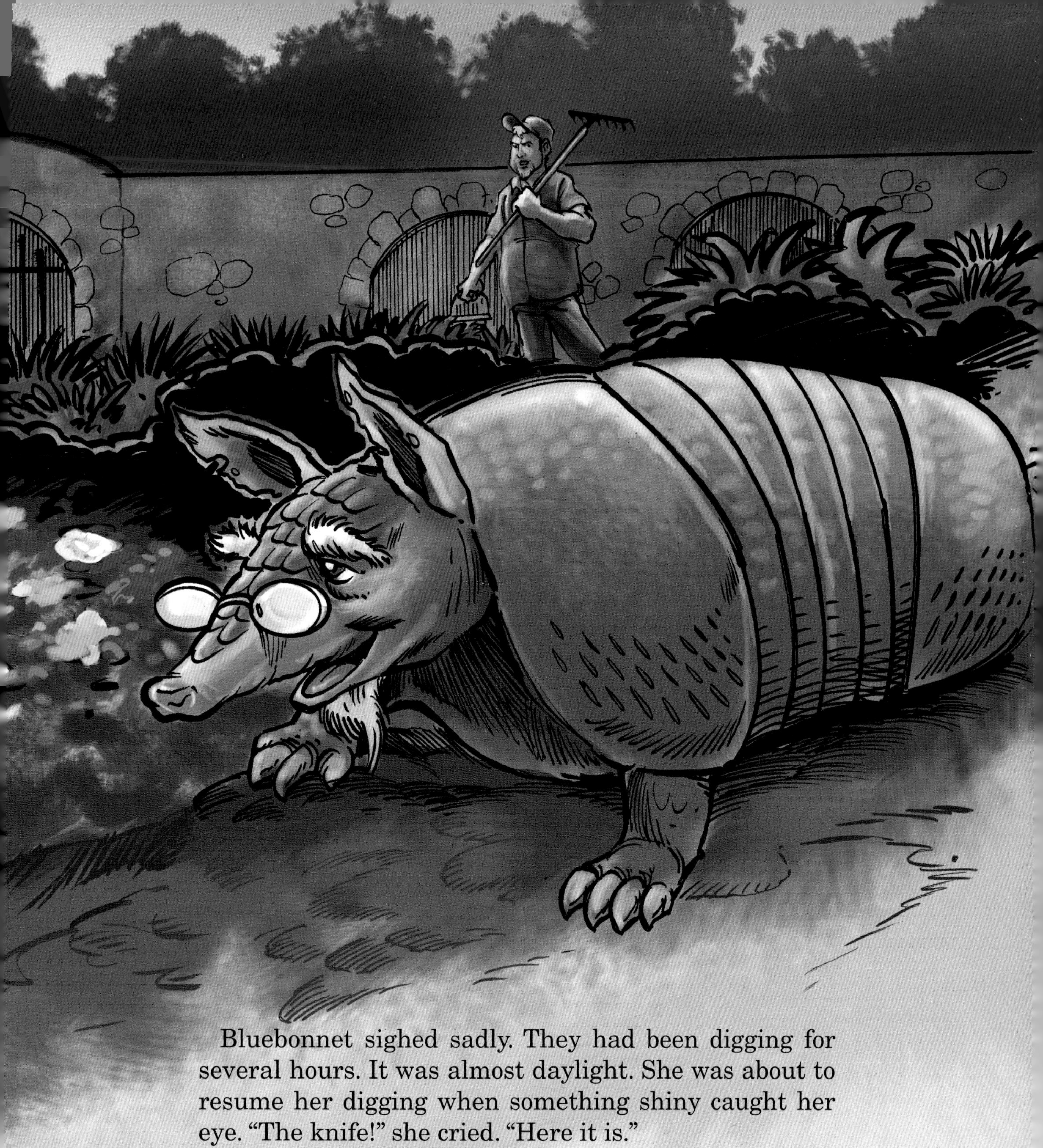

Bluebonnet sighed sadly. They had been digging for several hours. It was almost daylight. She was about to resume her digging when something shiny caught her eye. “The knife!” she cried. “Here it is.”

“Well, it appears to be all right,” he said, inspecting his prized possession carefully. “And it’s a good thing, too. What would Great-Great-Grand-Diller have thought about the Bowie knife being lost, after he rescued it from the battle?”

Bluebonnet frowned.

“Oh, well,” said Digger Diller, feeling a bit sorry for her. “The knife has been found again and . . . ”

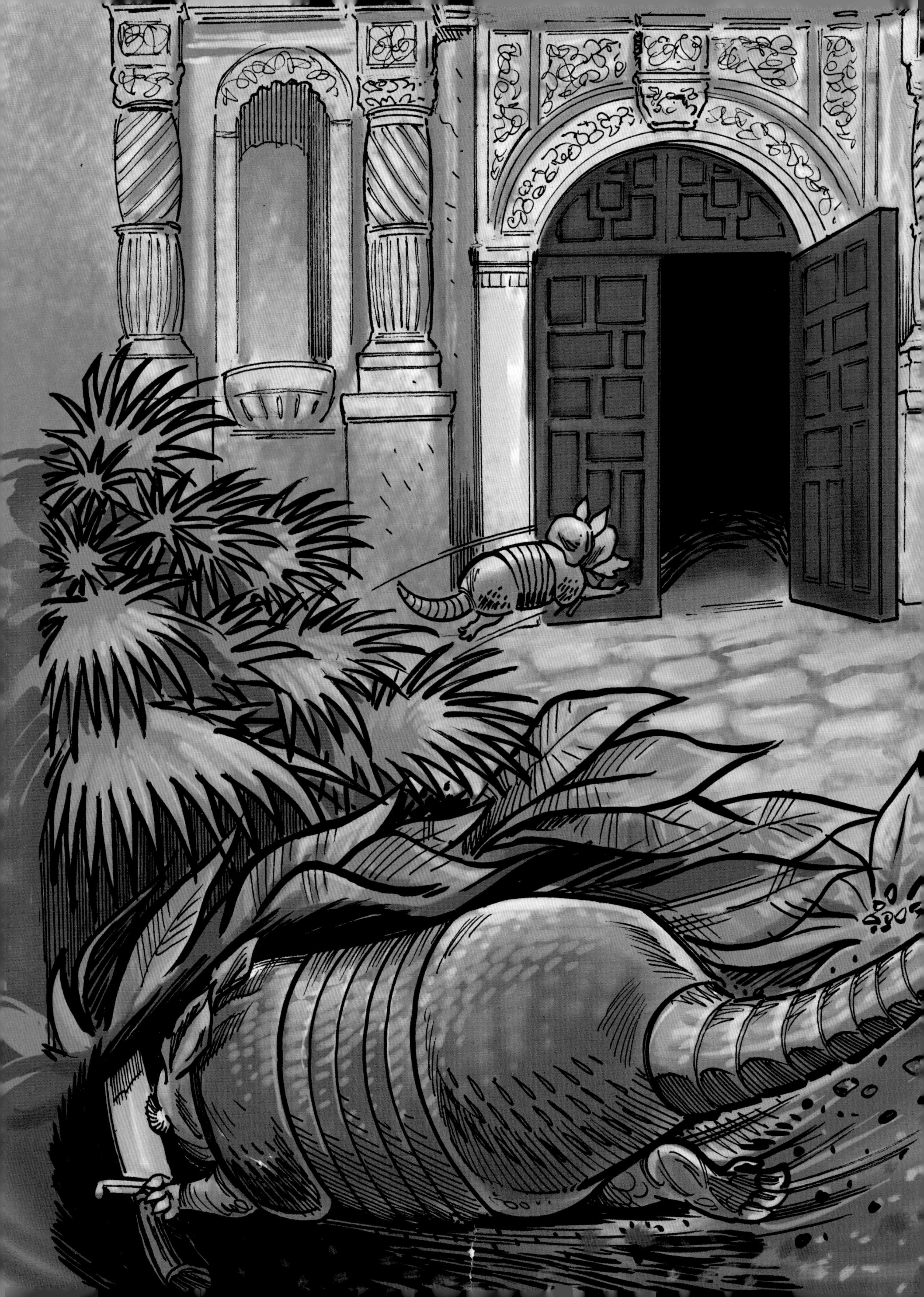

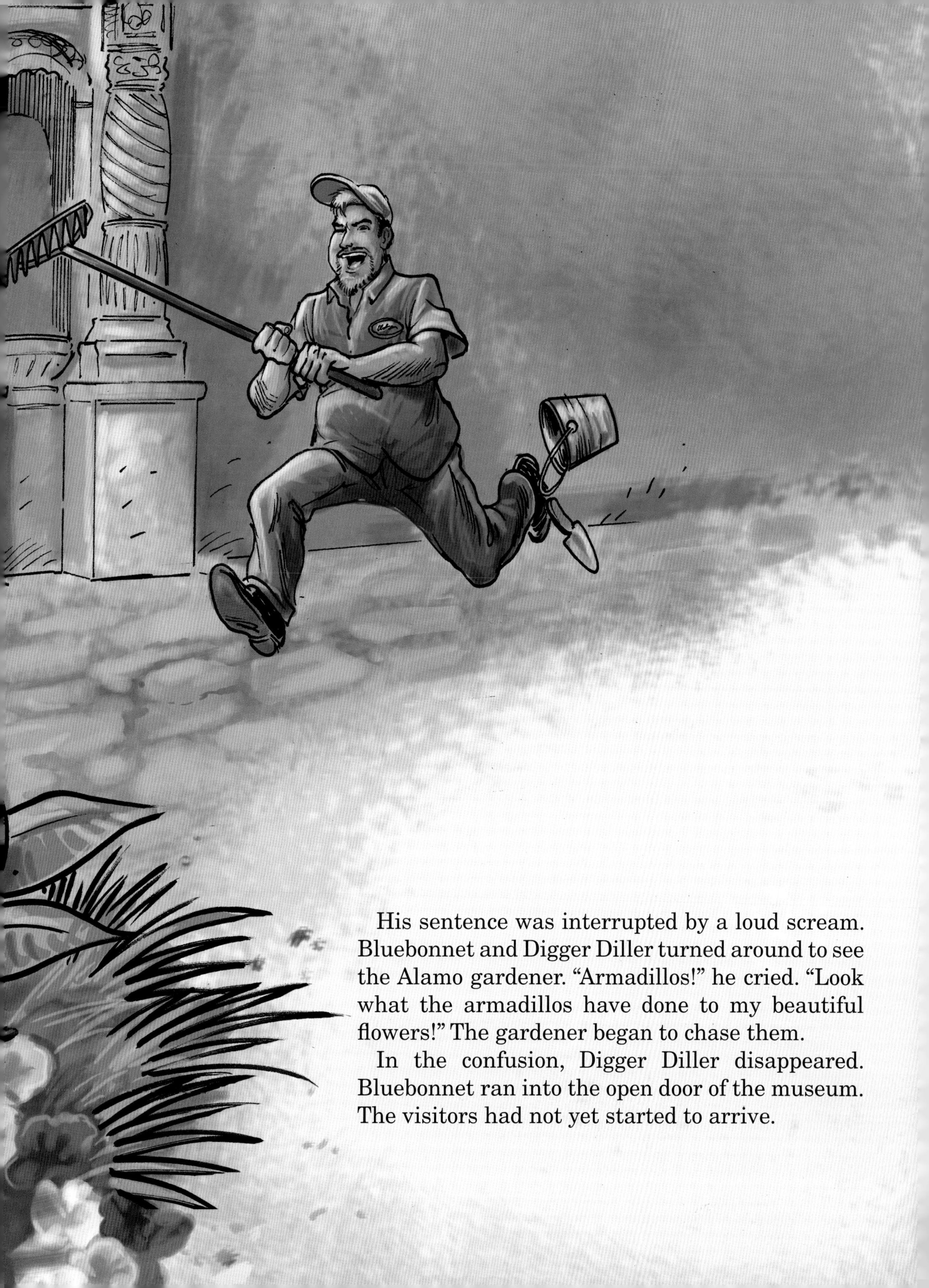

His sentence was interrupted by a loud scream. Bluebonnet and Digger Diller turned around to see the Alamo gardener. "Armadillos!" he cried. "Look what the armadillos have done to my beautiful flowers!" The gardener began to chase them.

In the confusion, Digger Diller disappeared. Bluebonnet ran into the open door of the museum. The visitors had not yet started to arrive.

Quietly, she peered into the display cases. She looked at the artifacts and read about the brave heroes of the Alamo, among them William Barret Travis, Davy Crockett, James Butler Bonham, and Jim Bowie. Bluebonnet was inspired by this shrine to their sacrifice.

"This would be the best place for the Bowie knife," she said with a sigh. "But Digger Diller will never agree to it now—not after the knife was almost lost."

Suddenly she heard the gardener's footsteps. Bluebonnet played dead!

"Well, at least I've got one of the culprits who dug up my flowerbed!" said the gardener, walking toward her. But Bluebonnet jumped up and ran out of the museum door.

"Come back here!" yelled the gardener, running after her.

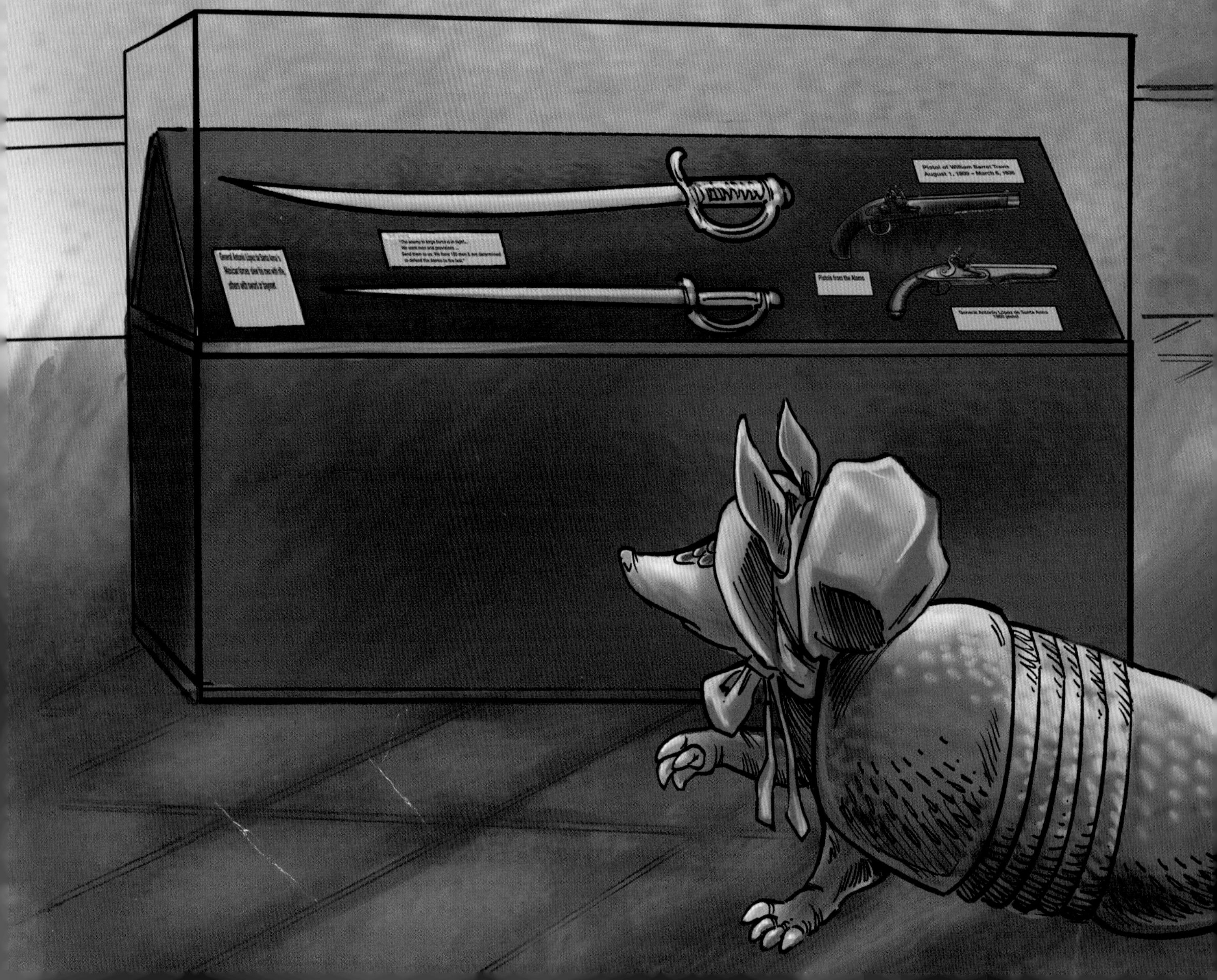
Pistol of William Barret Travis
August 1, 1809 – March 6, 1836
Pistols from the Alamo

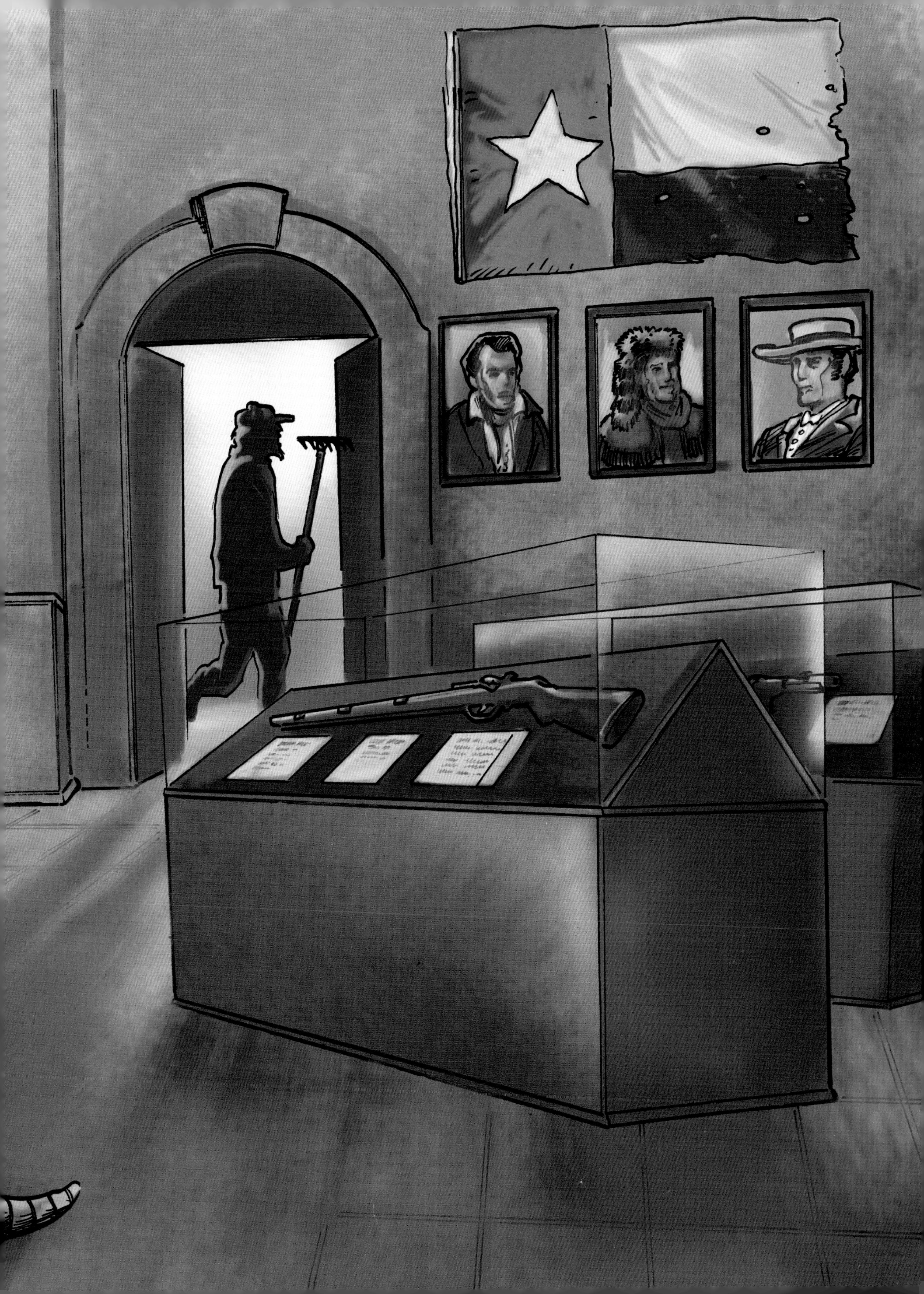

"Over here, Bluebonnet!" Digger Diller called.

She ran as fast as she could and tumbled into his den. "Oh, dear!" said Bluebonnet, trying to catch her breath. "That was close. But at least I saw the museum. Have you ever been in the museum?"

"Of course," said Digger Diller, a bit irritated by such a question. "As I told you, I've lived here all my life. I have been there many times."

Bluebonnet summoned all of her courage and said, "I still think the best place for Jim Bowie's knife is the Alamo Museum."

"How dare you suggest that idea again!" cried Digger Diller. "That knife, the pride of the Diller family, was almost lost because of you. And you want me to try to give it away again? Never!"

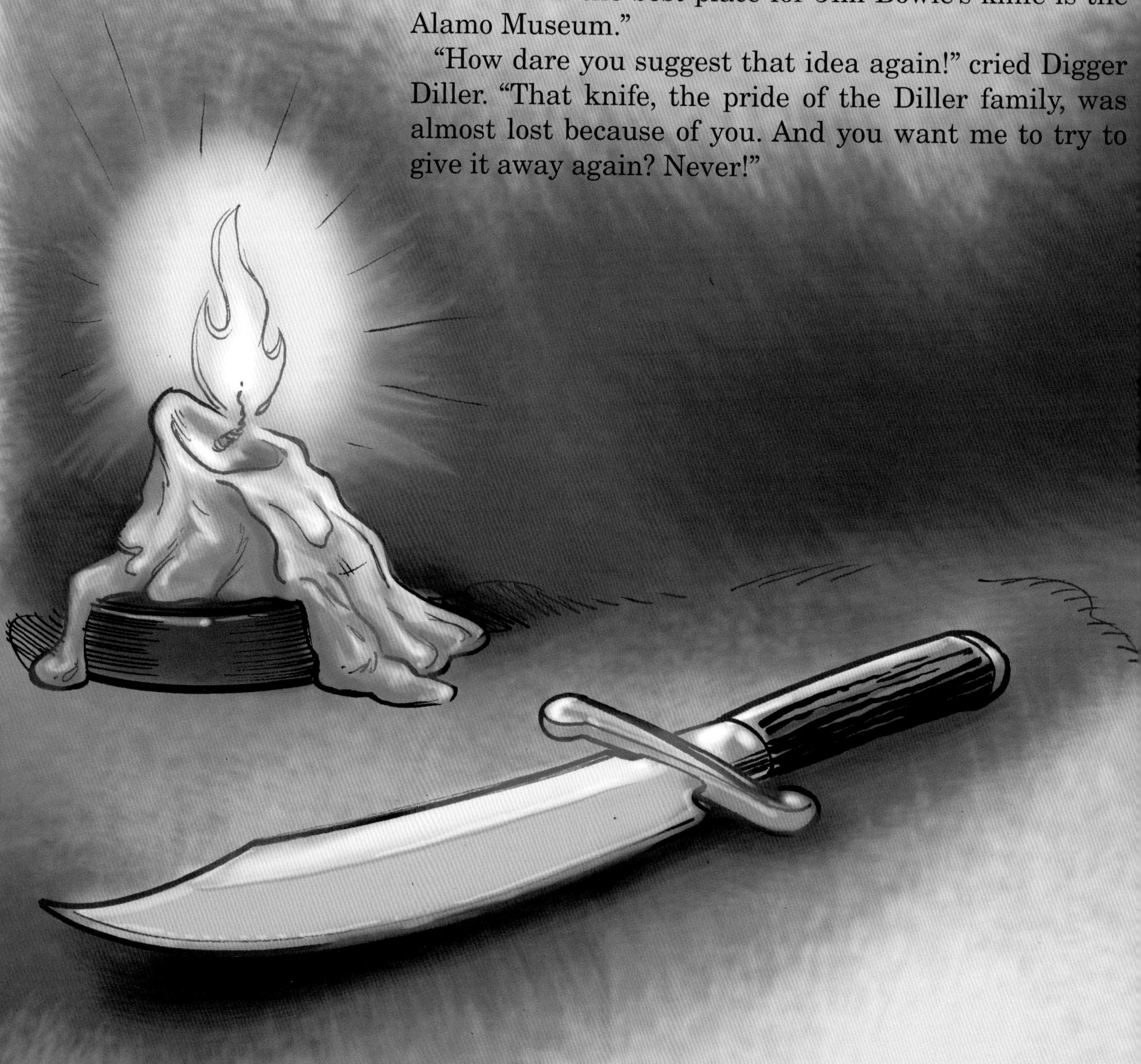

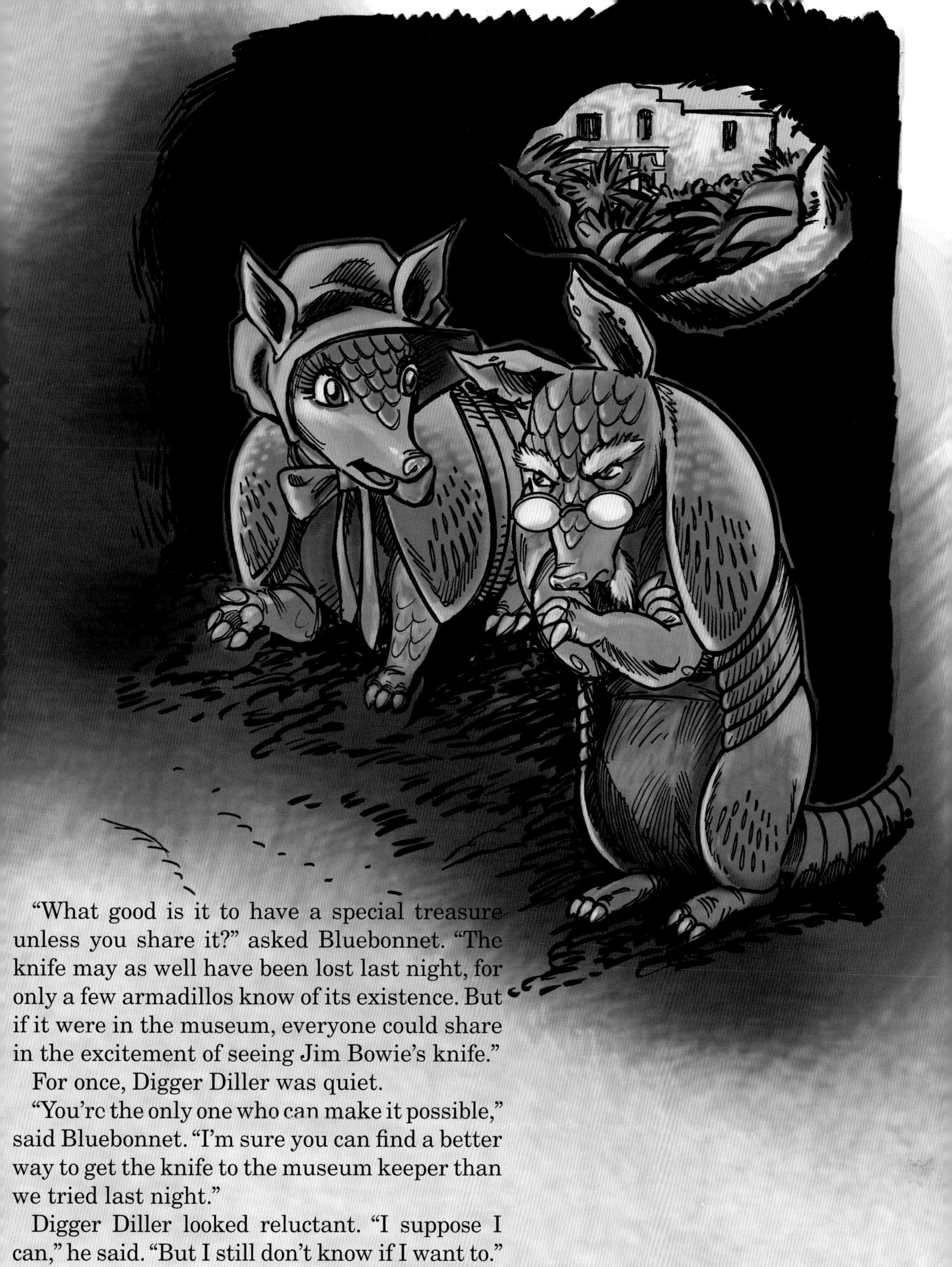

“What good is it to have a special treasure unless you share it?” asked Bluebonnet. “The knife may as well have been lost last night, for only a few armadillos know of its existence. But if it were in the museum, everyone could share in the excitement of seeing Jim Bowie’s knife.”

For once, Digger Diller was quiet.

“You’rc the only one who can make it possible,” said Bluebonnet. “I’m sure you can find a better way to get the knife to the museum keeper than we tried last night.”

Digger Diller looked reluctant. “I suppose I can,” he said. “But I still don’t know if I want to.”

Bluebonnet smiled at him. "You'll figure out the right thing to do," she said. She poked her head out of the burrow. The gardener was busy replanting flowers. Now was the time for her to leave. "Goodbye, Digger Diller, and thanks," she said.

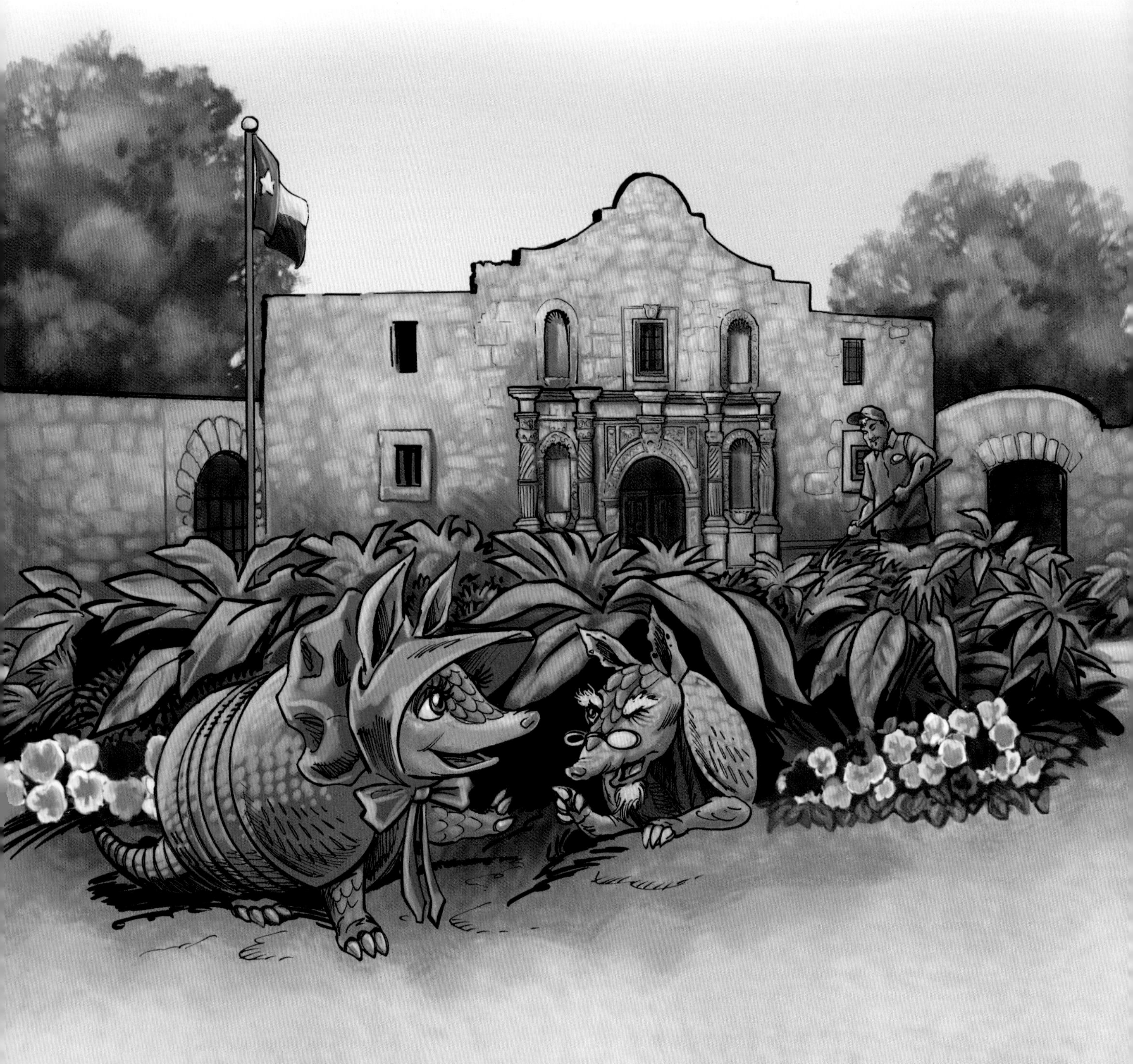

"Always 'Remember the Alamo!'" he called after her. And Bluebonnet promised she would.